SWEETWATER

A NOVEL BY JASON HEATON

swimpruf
PRESS

Published by Swimpruf Press, Minneapolis
www.swimpruf.com

First Edition, October, 2023

Cover design by Paul Andrews.

SWEETWATER

+

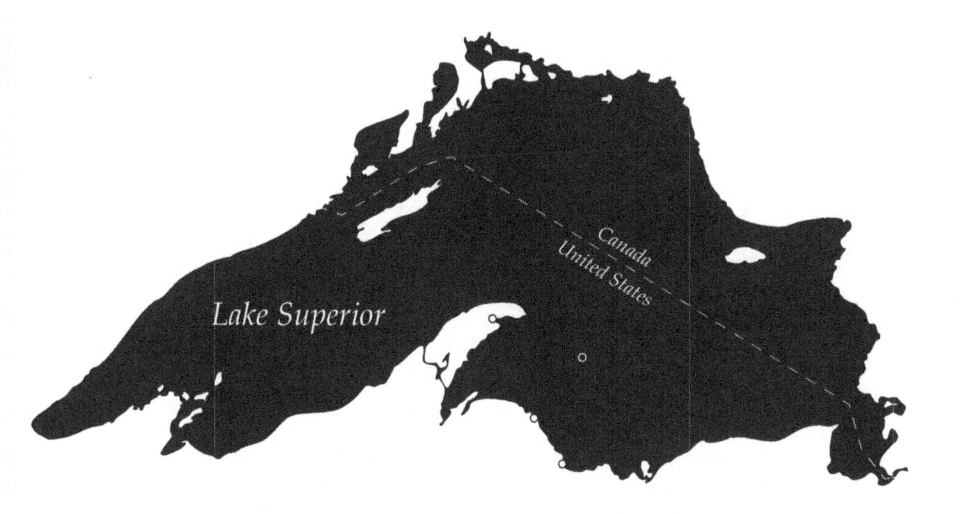
Lake Superior
Canada
United States
100km

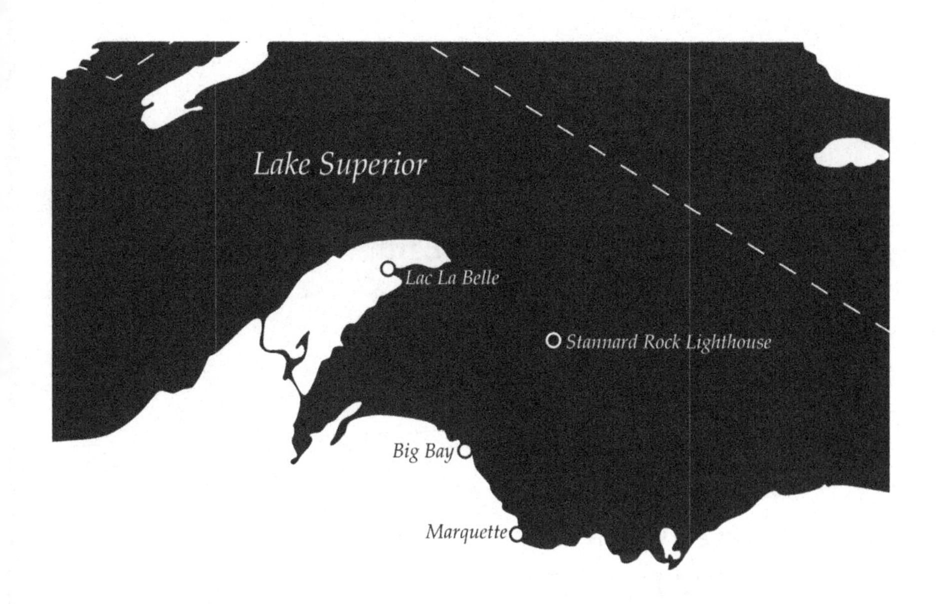
Lake Superior
Lac La Belle
Stannard Rock Lighthouse
Big Bay
Marquette
50km

Contents

SWEETWATER

This one's for the dads,
mine and all the others who make an effort.

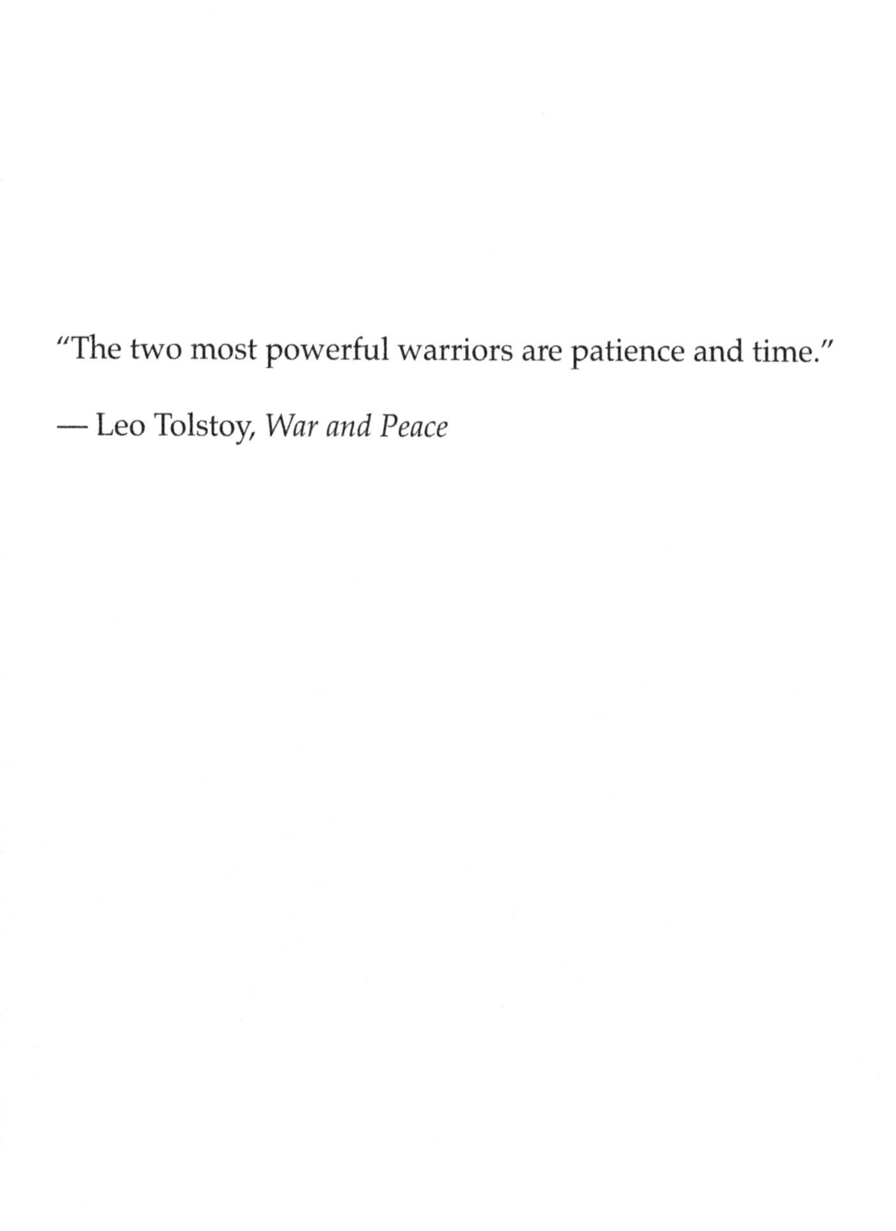

"The two most powerful warriors are patience and time."

— Leo Tolstoy, *War and Peace*

SWEETWATER

Prologue

Lake Superior, 44 nautical miles north of Marquette, Michigan. November 2nd, 1978.

Just south of the invisible Canadian border, high over Lake Superior, the Gulfstream II dipped its left wing and began its slow arcing descent. The pilot's voice came on the cabin intercom, with the archetypal confident drawl of every airline pilot in America.

"This is Captain Jaeger speaking. We've been cleared for landing in Marquette, so I need everyone to take your seats and buckle up. It might be a bit of a sporty landing. This is Michigan in November after all." There was a smattering of chuckles in the half-occupied main cabin.

"Senator, if you don't mind taking your seat, we're beginning our final approach," the flight attendant said, gesturing to the leather window seat in Row 1. She'd waited as long as she could before interrupting the man standing in the aisle.

"Of course, Miss," Senator Clay Overbrook said with a disarming smile, "safety first." It was one of his skills, making everyone feel important and respected. The flight attendant thanked him and returned to her own jump seat in the front galley. Overbrook had been leaning on two seat backs, holding court with a small group of journalists. His pale blue tie was loosened at his neck, collar open below his stubbled chin, shirt sleeves rolled up. He would have appeared the perfectly styled image of the working man's hero if he wasn't, in fact, so authentic already.

"We'll continue this conversation once we're on the ground," he said to the reporters, who were stubbing out cigarettes and tucking notebooks into briefcases. The senator slid back into his own seat, ran his fingers through tousled, curly black hair and looked out the window at the early evening darkness. The chartered plane had broken through the thick cloud deck and moisture streamed across the Perspex, blurring the view. Not that he could see a thing, but he knew that the lights of Marquette wouldn't be far ahead. He was looking forward to being off this plane and in his own bed for a change.

It had been a bruising campaign. Overbrook liked Jimmy Carter but two years of high inflation and unemployment laid bare his party to attacks, and the smug young Republican candidate, Ted Hockenheimer, had gained ground in the weeks leading up to this midterm election. Hockenheimer had come out of the Navy and was a rising star in his party. Now he had Overbrook's Senate seat in his crosshairs.

Marquette would be a friendly crowd. This was Overbrook's hometown. Though the local economy was suffering from a declining mining industry, the incumbent senator was preaching an upbeat message of reinvention. He proposed turning this former industrial region into a tourist economy, blessed as it was with ample skiing, watersports and other outdoor activities on offer. His choice of the derelict ore dock on the waterfront as a venue for tomorrow's speech was a symbolic one. He was about to announce a proposed spending bill that would partially fund the huge structure's transformation into a public park, providing hundreds of new jobs. He smiled to himself and swallowed the last of his Stroh's beer.

Out the window, the dark sky cleared and he thought he saw a bright flash. He strained his eyes and pressed close to the window. A lake freighter? There it was again. He leaned over and called out to the seated flight attendant, who was facing him in her seat, "Miss, do you know what this bright light is out in the lake?"

"That's probably Stannard Rock," she replied, "the old lighthouse. You only see it if you approach Marquette from the north."

Overbrook nodded and looked back out the window. That would explain it. This wasn't his usual flight from D.C. back to Michigan, but from a trade delegation visit to Ottawa. The light was gone in a cloud bank. Then, another flash, this one much, much brighter. And closer.

Stannard Rock Lighthouse has been called, "The Loneliest Place in the World," and the nickname is well deserved. Constructed in 1877 to warn ships off the shallow rock reef for which it is named, the 102-foot high tower is the most remote of any coastal lighthouse in the United States. It lies twenty-five miles from the nearest land mass, tiny Manitou Island, and forty-four miles from mainland Michigan.

Keepers stationed on Stannard were dropped off by the Coast Guard with enough supplies to last for months. In the early days they had no contact with the mainland until they were picked up at the end of their rotation. Lake Superior's notorious weather lashed the rock from every direction, waves sometimes freezing to treacherous ice even during the light station's short operational season from March through December. After a fire in 1961, the lighthouse was left unmanned, making it even lonelier.

The big man in the peacoat crouched out of the wind and pulled back his sleeve. He was wearing a pair of fingerless woolen gloves, and with his meaty right index finger he pressed a button on a cheap Casio watch. The weak backlight illuminated the screen: 6:32 p.m.. *Any minute now*. He pulled a wool watch cap down over his tangled mop of black hair. His exposed face was raw and red, his bulbous nose a tangle of broken blood vessels. His exhalations had frozen his unkempt beard into a mask of ice and frozen mucus. Despite his apparent misery, he didn't really mind the cold. He'd grown up in weather much colder than this. He stomped on the soggy cigar butt he'd been nursing for the past hour and took a final pull on a flask of vodka, sliding it into the inside pocket of his coat. He was eager to get on with the unpleasant mission and be off this godforsaken rock where he'd been camped, alone, for two days.

Above the noise of the wind and the crash of waves below the crib, he heard the distant sound of a jetliner high above. *Finally*. The pilot was throttling power up and down as he adjusted his final approach trajectory; the man knew this by now, after weeks of practice and reconnaissance. He stepped around the base of the lighthouse into the full force of the wind. His eyes teared up from the cold air. The rhythmic flash of the beacon a hundred feet above him briefly illuminated the crib, and he had this ridiculous thought that suddenly he'd be seen. But by whom?

The man shook his head and stepped to the edge of the railing. There, he bent and unzipped a long canvas duffel bag and pulled out the 9K32 Strela-2. He stroked the length of it admiringly, then, with a grunt, he shouldered the thirty-three pound launch tube and waited. Now he saw the plane coming over him, its navigation lights blipping in the black sky. "Red for port, green for starboard, just like on a ship," the man thought. He swung the tube up and peered down its length, through the iron sight at the business end. The fact is, he really didn't have to aim precisely. The Strela used infrared tracking. As long as he fired in its general direction after the plane passed, the missile would home in on the heat exiting the Gulfstream's two Rolls-Royce turbofan engines mounted at the aft end of its fuselage. He applied a half-trigger of pressure, allowing the missile to uncage and track a target. It was just as he'd done a hundred times in training in the empty forests across the lake in Ontario. A red light illuminated through the sights and a buzzer rasped, indicating it had locked on. He squeezed the trigger fully and felt the missile release with a kickback he knew well.

It worked perfectly. Soviet design is not pretty, but it is brutally effective. The missile streaked away, found its target in the cold sky and turned, as if with an intelligence all its own, until it bore into the left engine and exploded. The direct hit took off the entire tail of the plane. Without power or any means to control its yaw, the plane fell out of the sky like a meteorite. The man smiled grimly as he watched it plummet in a twisting arc of fire. He didn't bother to watch it hit the water, but instead ducked back out of the wind, setting down the launch tube and pulling out a fresh cigar. He cupped his hands to light it and savored the first draws on the Cohiba he'd been saving for this moment. Then, with the thick roll of Cuban tobacco firmly jammed in his teeth, he walked to the edge of the crib and heaved the launch tube over the side, into the crashing waves below.

The last thing Senator Clay Overbrook thought about before the Gulfstream nose-dived into the lake was not his family, or the end of his own life, but that now Ted Hockenheimer would win the election, and it made him sad. While the rest of the passengers were screaming, and luggage was tumbling out of the overhead bins, the senator made eye contact with the terrified flight attendant and smiled, as if to say, "everything's going to be alright." But it wasn't.

The plane fell 10,000 feet in less than a minute, corkscrewing in like one of the many mallards Overbrook had winged on his annual fall hunting trips in the Keweenaw Peninsula. It hit the water with such force that the nose crumpled back into itself and then continued to plunge underwater. The fuselage buckled like an accordion, breaking into three pieces as it sank. All three sections spiraled down into the dark, cold lake, coming to rest 190 feet deep like a child's broken toy. The tail though, had disintegrated from the impact of the missile, its debris scattered over miles of water.

The pilot and first officer were thrown clear of the cockpit on impact, their bodies never to be found. But the rest of the passengers and crew remained dutifully buckled in their seats—five journalists, two campaign staff members, three cabin crew, and Senator Clay Overbrook. A giant of the U.S. Senate, and some say its last true liberal voice, was dead.

The Pompeii of the Caribbean

Port Royal, Jamaica.
Present day.

With every breath, he was blinded, over and over. He closed his eyes and let the tropical sun color his vision blood red through his eyelids. The water cascaded off his shoulders and he took deep, rhythmic breaths, gulping in air with each turn of his head.

Every morning since arriving in Port Royal, Julian "Tusker" Tusk waded in off the dirty strip of sand and swam for an hour. He didn't know how far he was swimming, nor did he care. He simply swam parallel to the shore, out over the ragged reef of dead coral, using the distinctive, green-painted beach bar and the rotted pylons of the destroyed jetty as landmarks on shore. Then back and forth, again and again.

Scuba diving had been work for Tusker since his days in the underwater archaeology PhD program at Michigan Tech, so he relished these moments, nearly naked and alone in the sea. Without the false sense of protection a tank and dive gear lent, he enjoyed the feeling of vulnerability, swimming over deep water in just a pair of trunks and a dive mask.

He saw movement thirty feet below and stopped swimming. It was a sharp-nosed eel, the same color as the sand, with a viper's arrow-shaped head. Its pale white spots matched the dappled sunlight perfectly. It was rooting around under a flat shelf of dead coral, jabbing in and out, then curling around and trying a new angle of approach. A bar jack, with its distinctive electric blue stripe, hovered nearby, hoping to gain an easy meal if the eel flushed a small fish or crustacean into the open.

Tusker sucked in a few lungfuls of air and slowed his heart rate, then jack-knifed down with a duck dive and two powerful kicks. He wiggled his jaw to equalize the pressure in his inner ears and leveled off just above the eel, which showed him no interest and continued its hunt. Tusker always marveled that creatures that would seem terrifying on dry land seemed benign underwater. Sharks were like wolves, eels like serpents, yet he approached them without fear, coming within inches of them as they patrolled a reef or a wreck.

As his bloodstream accumulated carbon dioxide, he felt the familiar spasm of his diaphragm and with one last look at the eel, he turned for the air above. He let himself rise with no hurry, breaking the surface, exhaling to push the spent air from his lungs before deeply drawing breath.

He paused to get his bearings, lightly treading water with only his head and neck above the surface. His swim had followed a meandering path, veering out and away from shore instead of parallel to it, and he noticed that he was getting close to the reef's edge. A little ways out, two men with masks and snorkels were bobbing at the surface.

Every now and then, one would disappear beneath the surface, then reappear a few minutes later. Spearfishmen, after snapper or, if they were lucky, a barracuda. Compared to the indiscriminate net fishing more often practiced, it was more sustainable, but incredibly difficult to haul in enough to sell at the market, much less feed a family.

A small skiff with a buzzy outboard motor roared by, dangerously close. He heard a shout from its owner in an undecipherable Jamaican patois. Tusker squinted at his wristwatch: 7:45. Time to head in. The team would be assembling for breakfast soon.

Tusker had been in Jamaica for three months, leading a field research project on the sunken city of Port Royal. A handful of his graduate students from Michigan Tech were rotating through, as well as those from the University of the West Indies, and two archaeologists from Jamaica's Ministry of Culture. The goal hadn't really been new discoveries, but rather to give valuable field experience to the crop of new underwater archaeologists under Tusker's tutelage. Still, the discovery of a church bell and some coins had created a minor international stir, and further surveying of the vast "pirate city" was proving valuable for future research.

Port Royal had been a bustling maritime port during the seventeenth century, when Britain and Spain were jockeying for dominance in the Caribbean. The British government had given free rein to privateers to forcibly board, plunder, and then sink Spanish ships, with the promise of wealth and land in its overseas colonies.

Port Royal, on the southeast coast of Jamaica, became the *de facto* fiefdom of one Henry Morgan, perhaps the most famous of these gentlemen pirates. Morgan was something of a benevolent dictator, and the city prospered under his rule with a bustling harbor that saw vigorous trade of sugar, rum, and coffee, along with ample, more sinful, commodities. The rising tide of Morgan's wealth, as the saying goes, raised all ships. Until it didn't.

On July 7th, 1692, a massive earthquake offshore cleaved off a huge section of the Jamaican island, and the resulting tsunami swallowed up the city and thousands of its residents. Overnight, Port Royal was, literally, underwater. Today, it is considered the "Pompeii of the Caribbean," and the expanse of shallow underwater dig sites is an ideal classroom for students of maritime archaeology.

Back in his room at the Port Royal Arms, Tusker swapped his wet swim trunks for a dry pair, toweled his shaggy, salt-bleached hair, and padded over to the small rattan desk in the corner. He opened his laptop and scanned his e-mail inbox for anything important, ignoring numerous messages with Michigan Tech addresses. He was about to close the laptop screen when a message caught his eye. The subject line simply said, "Your father." It was from someone named Leila Mansour. He vaguely recognized the name but wasn't sure from where. He clicked the message.

"Dear Mr. Tusk," it began. *"My name is Leila Mansour. I write for the Detroit Free Press and am researching a story about*

the 1978 crash of Senator Overbrook's plane for the upcoming anniversary commemoration in Marquette. I was speaking with Mr. Chester Basch, who told me he and your father worked as divers on the recovery of that airplane wreck. Mr. Basch told me you might be able to provide some background, given your family connection and your current line of work. Please get in touch as soon as possible. Best regards, Leila."

Chester Basch. That's a name I haven't heard in a while, Tusker thought. "Uncle Chester," he used to call him. He and Tusker's father had been members of the same Underwater Demolition Team in Vietnam and, later, the Navy's Mobile Diving and Salvage Unit. Funny that neither of them had ever spoken about the Gulfstream crash. Or 'Nam, for that matter, Tusker thought. He hadn't seen Chester since shortly after his dad died. He shrugged and shut his laptop.

The Port Royal Arms was a charming but rather tired old hotel that dated back to Jamaica's days as a British colony, when authors, actors, and disgraced politicians came to escape. The lobby had a few artifacts from its glamorous history—a menu signed by Ian Fleming, a few photos of Noel Coward canoodling with Marlene Dietrich—though today most of its guests were European backpackers and budget travelers. It maintained a reputation for good service and authentic island cuisine.

Over a breakfast of ackee and saltfish with fresh mango and three cups of Blue Mountain coffee, Tusker laid out the day's plans. The last of the Tech students were finishing up their two-week rotation. With an active hurricane season forecast, it was time to start wrapping up diving operations. In an effort to preserve one of the submerged building foundations they'd excavated, Tusker told the team to re-bury it.

"Seriously, Professor?" exclaimed Winston, one of the Jamaican students. "We just spent two weeks scraping that thing out." Some of the other students nodded and murmured in agreement.

"Well, now you've got a week to cover it up again," Tusker smiled. "The fact is, if we don't bury it and mark it, a hurricane will, and far less carefully." Winston rolled his eyes.

"We got our material samples and did our photogrammetric modeling, which were our goals," Tusker continued, unmoved by the protests. "It's not like our plan was to raise Atlantis. Remember, archaeology isn't all Indiana Jones stuff, looting tombs and pocketing gold statues. We're simply here to document what's there."

"Alright, let's get down to the boat," Tadzio, the program coordinator from the Ministry of Culture chimed in, clapping his hands sharply. The group started to disperse, with chairs scraping and cups clinking.

"Have you seen Ian?" Tusker asked Tadzio as they walked out together.

"My guess is he's nursing a wicked hangover," he winked. "I heard him come in just a few hours ago. Seems Jamaica agrees with him."

"We'll soon find out," Tusker laughed.

Ian Walsh, the Brit whom Tusker had met in Sri Lanka last year, had joined the project in Jamaica on Tusker's invitation. Despite the lasting effects of the decompression sickness from their last dive together twelve months earlier, he remained an excellent archaeologist, and agreed to run topside support for the Port Royal project. Tusker was glad to have his dry, English humor and his way of keeping unruly students in line.

When they got to the dock, Tusker was surprised to find Ian already on the dive boat, dressed in board shorts and a faded Deep Blue Dive Resort T-shirt with its sleeves cut off. He was barefoot. Ian rarely wore any footwear. His partially paralyzed leg was visibly atrophied. "Waiting on you, as usual," he called out to Tusker. Tusker smirked back.

"I heard you were out a bit late last night," Tusker said. "Charming the local ladies again?" Ian was a consummate bachelor and seemed to live by the "girl in every port" cliché.

"Flying home in a few days, gotta make the most of my time here," he replied, tossing off the bow line and pushing the boat away from the dock, with an ease that belied his injury.

They did three dives in the morning, rotating crews in the water every hour. Tusker supervised two of them, and Clarence, one of the archaeologists from the Ministry, oversaw the other. Over a lunch break of cold chicken sandwiches and ginger beer, eaten while bobbing at anchor, Tusker sat moodily in the corner of the boat, hiding from the tropical sun under the boat's flimsy canopy. He didn't eat much. Watching Ian banter with the students, his ruddy face creased by a crooked smile under a floppy brimmed hat, reminded Tusker of their time together in Sri Lanka. It was a bittersweet memory. There doing fieldwork, he'd lost an old friend, and gotten pulled into a complicated and dangerous adventure diving a sunken World War II ship. Ian got the bends, and Tusker almost died himself. He'd also met a woman, Samanthi. He had barely recovered from it all before landing in Jamaica. He absent-mindedly spun the red and blue bezel of his Seiko dive watch. Some days he wondered if he'd recovered at all. Ian saw him and shimmied over.

"Hear anything from Sam?"

"You're a mind reader, aren't you?" Tusker said with a forced smile. Just before boarding her flight from Michigan back to Sri Lanka, Samanthi had slid the Seiko off her own wrist and pressed it into his hand. She gave Tusker a sad smile. "Something to remember me by." Then she turned to go. He squeezed the heavy lozenge of steel in his palm and watched her present her boarding pass and disappear into the jetway. She never looked back.

"I'm sure she's still pining for you, mate," Ian jolted Tusker from his thoughts. "She didn't know what she had with you."

"Oh, I think she found out," Tusker replied bitterly. "I messed that one up, royally."

"Ah, nothing a few thirsty photos on Instagram won't cure," Ian joked. "She'll be so jealous, you'll find her at your door up there in… where? Minnesota?"

"Michigan," Tusker corrected him, though he knew Ian was needling him. He got the state wrong every time, intentionally. "And I don't think so." He stood up and clapped his hands.

"Alright, let's do two more dives then call it a day," he called out to the group. "I'll lead this one." He shouldered his dive cylinder, climbed onto the gunwale, spat in his mask, puffed on his mouthpiece, and backrolled into the lukewarm Caribbean.

The survey site was only about 30 feet deep and well-lit by the sun high in the tropical afternoon sky, but the runoff of sewage and detritus from nearby Kingston reduced visibility to only a couple of arm lengths. Tusker had warned the students that this necessitated strict buddy diving and care taken to stay close to the designated search grid under the support boat. He descended to the bottom and waited for all the divers to splash in and regroup on the sea floor before spreading out to work. Everyone knew their role and he was pleased to watch the well-choreographed process unfold—some divers with tape measures, some with excavation tools, another with a camera, all intent on their individual tasks.

After forty-five minutes, he glanced at his watch. At this shallow depth, their dives could be up to ninety minutes long. The excavating and silt kicked up by all the divers had reduced visibility to mere feet. It was like floating inside a ping pong ball. Tusker's mind started to drift again back to Sri Lanka. Jamaica was his first extended underwater time after those deep dives on the wreck of the *Vampire,* the claustrophobia of the hyperbaric chamber aboard the dive support vessel, *Depth Charge,* those divers who'd tried to kill him…

Suddenly he couldn't get a breath. He sucked on his regulator and got only a metallic taste, but no air. His heart raced. He reached out to find someone, anyone. The closest diver was one of the students, anonymous in his black dive suit, with his back to Tusker. Tusker kicked over to him and tore the mouthpiece from the diver, shoving it into his own mouth and pulling a huge breath. The other diver was knocked off balance, stumbling in the sand, kicking up more silt. The two of them thrashed in the whiteout as if wrestling.

The other diver managed to find his own backup air source and take a breath. He gripped Tusker by the shoulders and made eye contact. It was Winston, the Jamaican Ph.D. student. Tusker's eyes were as big and white as scallops. He slowly regained his composure, now horrified by his loss of control. He took a big breath and pushed away from the student, leaving his mouthpiece dangling in the water. He kicked for the surface, exhaling as he ascended, breaking the surface with a cascade of water. He gulped a breath of air.

The commotion roused Ian who had been dozing on the front deck of the boat. He pushed back the brim of his hat and squinted down at Tusker in the water. He was about to wisecrack when he saw something in Tusker's eyes.

"Help me get him into the boat," Ian said to the boat captain, a weathered, older Jamaican man with long gray dreadlocks. A lilting reggae beat emanated from the tinny radio on board. The captain grabbed Tusker's tank by the valve and heaved it into the boat. Ian leaned over and grabbed him by the back of his wetsuit and pulled. Tusker climbed clumsily over the gunwale and flopped into the bottom of the boat, his eyes shut, panting hard.

"Happened again, huh?" Ian whispered, leaning over, his face only a few inches from Tusker's.

"I… I just lost track of time. Ran my tank dry," Tusker mumbled. "Silly… rookie mistake." He rolled to his knees and sat up, peeling his wetsuit off his shoulders. He didn't make eye contact. But Ian was right, it had happened again. The panic attacks were becoming more frequent now. Tusker had thought the best way to get over whatever was wrong with him would be to just get back in the water. *Dive*. It was all he knew how to do. It's what his father had done, although look where that got him—bitter, brooding, and crippled.

By this time, the other divers had surfaced and were talking animatedly as they handed their gear up and climbed into the boat.

"What the fuck was THAT?" It was Winston. He bore

down on Tusker, livid. "You trying to kill me along with yourself?" Tusker raised a palm as if to calm Winston down. "This man is a danger to us all down there!" Winston kept on shouting, to no one in particular.

Ian shuffled forward, getting between Winston and Tusker and said in a calm, quiet voice, "Let it go, mate. I'm sure it was nothing personal, even if you are an arsehole sometimes." He deployed his disarming, crooked grin. Then, to the group, "Let's call it a day, eh? I don't know about you all, but I know at least two of us that could use some of Jamaica's finest mellow ganja." This elicited a few laughs. Tadzio shook his head in mock disapproval. Ian winked at Winston and patted him on the shoulder.

Tusker didn't talk to anyone on the boat ride back. He squatted in the front of the boat with his knees up, staring at the sun as it dropped to the horizon. *I've got to get a grip,* he thought. Back by the roaring outboard, he could see Ian talking quietly to Winston, gesturing with his hands a lot. Winston was nodding and cast an occasional glance towards Tusker.

Back at the dock, Tusker was the last off the boat. He shouldered his own wet dive kit and bypassed the shed where they stored all the tanks and gear, going straight towards the inn. Ian called out and tried to catch up, but with his limp, he had difficulty on the rough path.

"Gonna run away from a cripple?" he said. "Not very sporting of you, even for an American."

Tusker stopped and shook his head, allowing the smallest of smiles to break his stony expression. They walked slowly together back to Tusker's room. Tusker dropped his gear on the balcony, and he heard Ian pop the caps off two Red Stripes. He passed one over to Tusker.

"What happened to you over there…" Tusker knew he meant Sri Lanka, "would have affected anybody. In some ways, I got off easy by getting the bends." He gestured towards his legs. "Have you talked to anyone about it?"

Tusker shook his head and took a swig of the beer. "I mean, who would understand? I lost a close friend, and killed two guys with my bare hands… and even managed to lose the girl in the end." Tusker had dispatched two divers employed by a maniac dead set on recovering the ship's secret cargo.

"Well, that's more cos you're ugly, but…" Ian nudged him and clinked bottles. "But seriously, I think you've got a case of post traumatic stress. PTS to the D. You're not going to solve this on your own, I'm afraid. I saw plenty of guys in my unit come back from Afghanistan messed up. But a lot of them got help and have gone on to be just fine."

"I was not in a war, Ian," Tusker replied. "I'm a peace-loving archaeologist, for Christ's sake."

"I disagree," Ian said. "We all fight our own personal wars. All I'm saying is, find someone to talk to. I'm sure even back there in, where is it, Wisconsin, you can find at least one decent therapist?"

"Michigan," Tusker said with a laugh. "Yeah. maybe. God knows, if I keep on pulling this sort of shit," he gestured in the direction of the ocean, "I'm either going to kill someone, myself, or lose my job. I still might, if Winston kicks this one up the chain of command."

"No worries there, mate," Ian said softly. "I had a quiet word with Winston. He's cool. Now what do you say we go find something a little stronger than this weak beer?" Ian said, holding two fingers in an imaginary joint to his lips.

"Nah, man, you go. I'm messed up enough without adding weed to my chemistry," Tusker said, patting Ian on the shoulder.

"Rum!" Ian shouted. "I meant rum! They gotta have some good navy proof stuff on this island."

Tusker laughed. He would miss Ian when he flew back home in a few days. Then again, the Englishman was yet another reminder of the demons that haunted him. The sun had set and the night insects were starting their chorus. Somewhere below the balcony, a band started to play some old school reggae for the tourists. They finished their beers and went off to find a bottle of rum.

Ian never did tell Tusker that he checked his tank later and found that it wasn't even close to being empty.

Deep Dive

Marquette, Michigan.
Present day.

"Tell me about Jamaica," Dr. Cassandra Fuchs said. "What happened there?" It was a beautiful late October afternoon, the kind that reminds people why they live in a place where winter lasts seven months out of the year and summer only about two. Sunlight streamed through her office windows, and beyond, twinkled off the lake like thrown diamonds.

"As I said, it was a panic attack," Tusker shifted uneasily in his chair, one of those trendy Eames knockoffs. He wore a T-shirt from a Sri Lankan dive resort under a badly pilled old Patagonia fleece vest. He had the advantage of facing the windows and he looked past Dr. Fuchs, as if longing to be out on the water instead. "I used to get them when I was a teenager, but that was for…" he paused, "different reasons. It never happened to me while diving until this past year."

"What do you think brought them on when you were a teenager?" D.r Fuchs chased this new crumb. Tusker knew she would go there, and he regretted mentioning it.

"Social anxiety, I think they call it nowadays?" he said. "I was a fairly awkward kid, didn't really fit in. I was athletic, I guess, but not in the way that fit any mold. Not a 'jock,' didn't play team sports… I was more of a dreamer, always running around the woods, swimming, writing in a journal, that sort of thing." He laughed, nervously. "Not exactly social."

"Sounds like a pretty healthy childhood to me," Dr. Fuchs replied. "Did you have friends?"

"A couple." He looked out the window again, as if conjuring faces. "There was Tommy. He was more popular than me, and I think I was sort of an escape for him when he needed a breather from partying." Tusker uncrossed his legs, then reconsidered and re-crossed them. "Carl was who I guess you'd call my best friend. In a way, I think I idolized him."

"And why was that?" the doctor prodded gently. She appraised him over her notebook. He was not her typical patient. He carried himself confidently, without so many of the tics and fidgets of many of her anxiety patients, but seemed comfortable with vulnerability. He was also handsome, in the way of someone who doesn't know it—the unkempt hair, the stubble, the well-fitting but worn casual clothes. There was an ease with his lean, muscular physique, as if his body was more of a tool than something to attract women. Or men. She wasn't sure yet. Something to explore.

"What was it about Carl?" she asked.

"He just seemed so self-assured. Knew what he wanted to do and who he was. He was in a rock band, ran marathons, dressed like he didn't give a shit what anyone thought of him."

"That's difficult to do at that age."

"Yeah, but I guess it was all an illusion. He was a bit of a mess like the rest of us were. His dad beat the crap out of him, he told me later. He was borderline anorexic. He dropped out of college and started drinking a lot. This was after we'd lost touch for a few years."

The doctor scribbled in a notebook, then cleared her throat. Tusker observed her. He could be attracted to her if she wasn't so prickly. Her blond hair was tied back in a sensible high ponytail, and she wore a fitted cream turtleneck that showed off her lean physique. Her face was lined, probably from years outdoors. Tusker guessed runner, or probably skier and mountain biker, since this was Marquette.

"And how was your own relationship with your parents? They're both gone now, right?" she asked. He looked away quickly, self-conscious that he'd been staring.

"Yeah, Dad died when I was eleven. Mom just a few years ago." Tusker recalled those last days watching his mother waste away in the hospice wing of the nursing home. The cancer had eaten her from the inside out. He'd just made it home from an expedition in the Yucatán to say goodbye.

"I guess it was an OK relationship, more so with my mom

than my dad. He was pretty fried from Vietnam and his diving accident. Didn't say much. Taught me to dive though, even from his wheelchair." Tusker laughed and shook his head. "I was dead scared to breathe underwater but there he was, sitting on the dock, watching."

"Did you feel pressured to do it?" Dr. Fuchs asked.

"It wasn't so much pressure as it was, I guess, I really wanted to please him." Tusker fixed her gaze.

"And do you think you did?"

"It was hard to tell. He wasn't a very emotive man, let's put it that way." Tusker smirked. "But I guess watching me dive must have given him some satisfaction."

He recalled that abnormally hot summer day, standing on the dock at their cabin on Lac La Belle. He was wearing swim trunks and his father's dive mask, which was way too big for his face. It leaked badly when he was underwater, which, looking back, was probably intended by his father as some sort of test. He'd been afraid to jump in with the diving cylinder, its weight on his back making it almost impossible to even stand up, his father shouting from his wheelchair, calling him a "chicken." Finally he did jump in, surprised to find he could float, and then swim, and breathe underwater. The sight of the walleye hiding in the shadow of the dock fascinated him, the tiny minnows in the waving grass at the bottom like an alien species welcoming him to a different planet. He didn't mention any of this to Dr. Fuchs.

"Now that you're an adult, and given some of the traumas you experienced last year in Sri Lanka, has it helped you better understand what your father was dealing with. His own experiences in Vietnam, maybe?"

"I hadn't really drawn those parallels," Tusker replied. "But then that's why I'm paying you, I guess." He laughed abruptly and a little too loudly at his own joke. Dr. Fuchs smiled benevolently but said nothing. She was waiting for him to respond to her question. *She's good,* Tusker thought.

"Dad was from a different generation, when being a strong, silent type was some sort of male archetype," Tusker looked to see if Dr. Fuchs would respond to that bit of psychobabble. She didn't. He continued. "Since he didn't talk much at all about Vietnam, and I was too young to understand the war or his diving accident, I guess I'll never know. But I'd like to think I learned from him how to communicate better. He'd never have dreamed of doing this." Tusker paused. "Therapy, I mean."

"Maybe so," Dr. Fuchs replied. "The military wasn't as good back then at taking care of its own, in terms of mental health. But trauma is trauma, and regardless of how you deal with it, some of our core responses will never change. Fight or flight, for example." She twirled her pen as she spoke. To Tusker, it seemed an uncharacteristically whimsical action. She almost became animated.

"What happened to you in Jamaica was likely a learned

response, your body's way of protecting itself against something it had experienced before, in your case, underwater. It's no different than a dog snapping at people after being kicked too many times."

"Well, whatever it was, I need to solve it, because this is pretty much what I do. An underwater archaeologist who can't go underwater is just ballast." As soon as he said it, he thought of Ian, his own diving days cut short, and regretted saying it. After all, it was on Ian's prodding that he was here, for whatever that's worth.

"We'll get you there, don't worry," she said reassuringly. "We're only a couple of sessions in, here. Understanding the cause is our first order of business. I suppose it's like in your work, studying a shipwreck to find out why it sank."

"Are you calling me a wreck?" Tusker smiled. Dr. Fuchs flashed a broad smile and laughed out loud. Had she blushed? Suddenly, he liked her more.

"I'd like to explore your relationships a little more." She became serious once more, like a cloud passing over the sun. "You talked about your parents and a little about your childhood friends. I'm seeing a pattern: working out who you are as a man, and also seeking approval from your father."

Here we go, thought Tusker, *out comes Freud.*

"But I'm also curious about your romantic relationships with women... or men?" She asked the last part tentatively. "Last week you briefly mentioned someone with whom you were involved… Sam, was it?"

"Woman, definitely a woman," Tusker smiled. "If that's what you're tiptoeing around. Sam was short for Samanthi, by the way." He unconsciously spun the bezel of his… Sam's—dive watch.

"Glad we cleared that up," Dr. Fuchs smiled, "And why do you think that relationship ended?"

"Pick a reason," Tusker said, his tone turning bitter. When Sam came back to Michigan with Tusker, he could almost envision a future, a real future, out as far as the mind's eye could see. It was the first time he'd even considered settling down with someone, a reason to slow down, maybe plant a garden, give up some of the fieldwork that had him traveling six months out of the year. But looking back now, they'd both been running away from something, not towards something. And it caught up with them.

"Mostly my fault," he mumbled. "Things were OK for the first month or so. We needed some space from what we'd both been through, and here…" he gestured out the window, "was about as far from all that as we could get."

"But not far from what you both carried inside," Dr. Fuchs said softly, sensing Tusker's change in mood.

"More me than her. We shared a couple of near-death experiences, but she couldn't know what I was dealing with, having to take someone's life…" His voice trailed off, then he sat forward and looked at Dr. Fuchs. "It's just not normal."

"Did you try to explain it to her?"

"Not as well as I could have, I suppose."

"You were a soldier, in a war..." Dr Fuchs offered.

"That's what Ian said, but it's not what I signed up for. I'm a scientist, for God's sake!"

"Maybe you understand your father a little better now."

"Maybe." He said it with a finality that signaled he was ready to stop talking about it.

"We'll leave it there for today," Dr. Fuchs said, looking at her own watch, a pebble-shaped gadget on a perforated rubber strap. "That's about an hour."

Tusker stood up and brushed imaginary crumbs from the front of his pants.

"I'm going to give you a little homework before next time," the doctor said with a small smile. Tusker didn't reply. She continued anyway.

"Try to get to know your father better. Maybe look through old family photos, mementos, anything. Forgive him, empathize with him. It might help you forgive yourself a little too. And that's what we're after."

Tusker nodded with a weak smile. Then he turned and walked out of the office into the bright, crisp autumn afternoon. There were booths set up at the park around the old ore dock on the lakefront, with people selling crafts and late season vegetables. Live music was playing somewhere. He thought of Sam and how she had loved autumn, how they built fires at the cabin, how she wore his sweaters and took to single malt. He shook his head as if to get rid of the memories and broke into a jog back to his car. He had a three-hour drive home ahead of him, and the sun set early.

The Keweenaw

Lake Superior.
Present day.

A week after the First World War ended, three identical minesweepers steamed away from the Canadian Car and Foundry shipyard in Fort William, Ontario. They had been built on spec for the French Navy, and were headed for the far side of the Atlantic via the St. Lawrence Seaway. But on their maiden voyage, they had to cross all five of the Great Lakes.

On November 18th, 1918, a gale blew up on Lake Superior as *Inkerman, Cerisoles,* and *Sebastapol* passed the Keweenaw Peninsula of northern Michigan. Facing huge waves and hurricane force winds, the ships became separated, and while *Sebastapol* narrowly escaped, the other two minesweepers were lost without a trace. All hands were lost—76 French sailors and two Canadian captains—making their combined sinking the single largest loss of life on Lake Superior. The ships have never been found.

It was late in the season to be on the big lake in a small survey boat. Though the late October sun still had some warmth, the wind was from the north and had been blowing across the water all the way from Canada. With its chill, it also brought long, rolling swells that lifted the R/V *Keweenaw* up and down as she idled over 250 feet of water.

Tusker stood out of the wind in the cabin's doorway, explaining the day's goals to his small crew of three PhD students. He was dressed in a pair of old jeans, a wool commando sweater, and a pair of badly neglected Blundstone boots. The students were kneeling at the stern, getting ready to deploy the side-scan sonar off the rolling transom. One of them, a bearded Texan named Logan, was struggling to keep his breakfast down.

"There's no shame in being green, Logan," Tusker said with a wry grin. "Just be sure to lean outboard, or you'll be swabbing the decks." The poor kid nodded under his baseball cap.

"The trick is to time your release with the swells," Tusker called encouragement to the students. "You want to toss it in when we're at the top of a swell, not the bottom. Otherwise, it'll just end up getting thrown back onto the transom." Logan looked at him. "The towfish, not your breakfast, just to clarify." The captain, an Irish transplant named O'Connell, was leaning on the console in the small cabin, eating a sandwich he'd brought along, and he looked up and chuckled.

Sarah, another student, was standing on the transom, which was awash in green water. She was wearing fishing waders and a heavy fleece jacket under a foul weather shell. She was a "Yooper," a lifelong resident of the U.P.,

Michigan's Upper Peninsula, and the most comfortable of the three in the challenging conditions. She was checking the winch spool, making sure the sonar's cable wouldn't get fouled as it was paid out.

Ming was from Malaysia, and in the final month of his PhD. Nothing ruffled him and he was busy checking the connections on the torpedo-shaped towfish. He'd already turned in his final thesis— something about the effects of climate change on the condition of freshwater shipwrecks— and today was more for fun than any sort of requirement. Tusker was glad to have his quiet competence along.

With a final check, and with the *Keweenaw* riding the crest of a roller, Logan and Sarah pitched the towfish into the water. Ming released the catch on the winch spool and nodded to O'Connell, who slowly pushed the throttles forward. The boat moved off, trailing the towfish, which sunk beneath the surface. Logan immediately leaned over the gunwale and wretched. Everyone looked away, glad to be moving finally. The idling boat, with swirling wind circulating its exhaust fumes, combined with the rolling swells, was enough to make the hardiest sailor a bit peaked.

Sarah, Ming, and Tusker settled in under the canopy at the open rear of the cabin, while Logan took first shift minding the towfish cable. He was glad to be in the fresh air while the others stared at the laptop screen for anomalies—visual shapes that hint at something manmade on the lakebed, ideally a sunken French minesweeper—as the towfish passed over it. It went on like this for the whole morning, the students switching off duties on the boat, interspersed with breaks for coffee and calls of nature off the transom, Sarah dropping the tail of her bibs in front of the men without inhibition.

"Thought we might get lucky today," Ming said, rubbing his eyes after looking at the screen for an hour straight.

"There's a reason they haven't been found yet," Tusker replied. "Either they went down somewhere far from where everyone thinks they did, or they're living out quiet lives as fishing trawlers in the south of France right now," he grinned. O'Connell barked a hoarse laugh and fished a cigarette pack out of the pocket of his Carhartt jacket. He offered one to Tusker, who thought about it, then declined.

"But seriously, this is truly a needle in a haystack hunt," Tusker continued, recognizing a teaching opportunity. "Up until recently, all the searches had centered on the waters off of the Keweenaw Peninsula, but Professor Colquhoun has been analyzing the weather and currents and some reports from other ships in the area the day they went down, and he reckons they might have made it a bit further. All we can do is keep methodically expanding the search grid."

And so they did, into the afternoon, with no luck. Every time they came across a ship-shaped shadow on the sonar feed, Sarah or Ming or Logan would cross-reference the GPS coordinates with those of known wreck sites. Tusker could almost recite their names when he saw the shadows of them appear on the screen. Still nothing that looked like the lost minesweepers.

"Got something," Ming called out excitedly. He was pointing at the screen as a shape started to paint itself. It soon became apparent that it wasn't a ship. "That looks like... an airplane! See the wings?"

"A Gulfstream II to be precise," Sarah said matter-of-factly, after seeing the familiar swept-back wings.

Ming looked at her incredulously. "How do you know that?" he asked.

"My grandfather was on that plane." She looked out over the grey green water. "November of '78."

"Holy shit, I'm... I'm sorry," Ming said. She nodded and waved him off.

"I never knew him," she said. "He died before I was born."

Tusker had been listening to the conversation. "I didn't know that, Sarah" he said from his perch inside the pilothouse. "Why was he on that flight?"

"He was flying it," she replied. Now it was Tusker's turn to be shocked. Both he and Ming looked at her with mouths open. Even O'Connell turned and looked. No one knew what to say.

"The official NTSB report said it was 'pilot error' that caused the crash," Sarah's tone grew bitter. "But my mom says he was a scapegoat. Grandpa was a damn good pilot, apparently. Flew F-86 Sabres in Vietnam, and those were supposed to be *really* hard to land. Landing a Gulfstream at Marquette would have been a cakewalk for him."

Tusker didn't mention his own father's involvement in the salvage and investigation, but it occurred to him that they had both been affected by that crash.

"If any good came out of it though," she said, with a cheerful turn of tone, "that crash is what made me want to be an underwater archaeologist." She forced a smile. The shape of the plane had moved off of the sonar feed and the lakebed went back to an empty wasteland. They were suddenly lurched out of the somber conversation by the sound of Logan wretching over the side of the boat.

"I think Logan has had enough for one day," Tusker said and stood up. "Let's reel in the fish and head back to the dock. Live to sweep another day."

As the three students coiled the coaxial cable around its spool and secured the towfish in its Pelican case on the back deck, Tusker thought about what Sarah had said. That plane crash, in some ways, is what also made him want to be an underwater archaeologist. He just didn't know it at the time. O'Connell swung the *Keweenaw* around, now into the stiff breeze, and pushed the throttles to full. The boat slowly lifted its bow into the setting sun and headed west for home.

The Scout

Lac La Belle, Michigan.
Present day.

The old truck lurked in the back of the shed like a serial killer in a bad movie, waiting to pounce on an unsuspecting victim. Only it hadn't actually moved in over three decades. It just sat there, taunting Tusker. After his parents died, Tusker began to spend more and more time at the old family cabin on the shore of Lac La Belle. Then he moved there for good. It wasn't exactly convenient when he needed to teach at Michigan Tech—Houghton was an hour's drive away, and the closest big city, Marquette, over three. But he had grown to cherish the sounds of the wind, the loons, and the occassional wolf, especially after traveling around the world on expeditions.

The cabin had been built in the 1930s, a classic Northwoods lake house with post and beam construction, a screen porch at the back, stone fireplace in the main room, and a removable dock down at the lake. Jonathan Tusk had added the oversized shed for his truck, tools, and his dive gear. The whole property had seen better days, but Tusker was slowly working to renovate it. And now it was time to get the Scout running.

"The moment of truth," Tusker called from the driver's seat, and twisted the key. The starter motor engaged, the engine hesitated, then turned over. But it didn't fire. "Damn."

"I still think it's the carb," Carl Sommers backed away from under the hood. He wiped his hands on the front of his faded coveralls and put a cigarette between his lips.

Tusker climbed out of the cab and animatedly waved his hand in front of his face. "You might want to do that outside." There was a strong smell of gasoline. "It's clearly getting fuel. Just gotta work out the fire and air part of the equation."

Carl looked at him through the flame of his old lighter, ignoring the warning. He snapped the lighter shut and drew smoke into his lungs, then exhaled luxuriously.

"You said you cleaned the jets and adjusted the float?" he asked, vaguely gesturing with the cigarette towards the engine.

"Yup," Tusker replied. "I rebuilt the whole thing. Though I wouldn't say it was an expert job. I should have just bought a new carburetor. That one's older than me."

Carl squinted at him and flicked ash onto the cracked concrete floor. "Let's spray some starter fluid right in the intake. If she starts, we'll know it's the carb." He walked over to the workbench, which was lit from above by a flickering fluorescent tube that cast a sickly pallor. The surface was covered with oily tools and various parts so that there was barely free space for Carl's beer can. He picked it up and took a swallow.

"Part of the problem is, we're drinking the wrong beer," he grinned and crushed the empty can for emphasis. "If you're gonna work on an old Scout, you can't drink this microbrew double IPA shit. Needs to be something old school. Leinie's or PBR. The truck knows the difference."

"Hey, Bell's is legit," Tusker shot back. Carl snorted.

In the early '70s, International Harvester introduced the Scout II, a replacement for the previous generation Scout 800. Still built in Fort Wayne, Indiana, it was seen as a badly needed update to its predecessor, but was only slightly less agricultural. Two doors, a bench seat, four-speed manual gearbox and two-speed transfer case were standard. You could order air conditioning and bucket seats, even cruise control back then, but Tusker's dad didn't want it that way. He just needed a simple truck to get him and his wife to the cabin in all weather. So he ordered the bone stock Scout II in the first year it came out, with the hard top and steel rims, painted in Ceylon Green, which bore no resemblance to its verdant namesake island, but was more of the color of dry grass.

After his diving accident in 1978, Jonathan Tusk stopped driving and the Scout sat where he'd last parked it, in the shed. When his son got older, Jonathan tried to get him interested in it, showing him how to change the oil and spark plugs, but he died before Julian was old enough to drive it. Since then, the old truck just sat in the dark, chewed and shat in by mice, who nested in the recesses of the engine bay and chassis. It held a dark aura there, reminding Tusker of his father and everything they'd left unsaid and unfinished. Then, one day he decided to get it running again— changed the fluids, put a new battery in, replaced the mouse-chewed wires. Now it was time to see if it would start.

Carl disconnected the air intake from the carburetor and held the plastic nozzle of the starter fluid can inside it. "Alright, crank it again."

Tusker climbed in and turned the key. The starter whirred, the engine turned, and Carl sprayed the flammable mist directly into the throat of the motor. It still didn't start.

"Shit," Carl said. The shed fell silent. "Well, then we're lacking *fire*. Grab a plug socket." He proceeded to pop the rubber wire boots off each spark plug. Tusker followed him with the socket and unthreaded the plugs, pulling them out of the engine block. They were dripping wet with gasoline and the smell was nauseating.

"I think we know our problem," Tusker said. "No spark."

"Early days of electronic ignition," Carl said. "I say we convert it back to points and a condenser, if you've got the parts." He pulled another cigarette out of his pack. Tusker's eyes widened in fear.

"Let's take that outside," he pointed to the door. Carl rolled his eyes and followed. "And give me one of those too."

"Uh oh, something's up if you're smoking," Carl said, eyeing Tusker and extending the open pack of Camel Lights in his direction.

"Nah, call it peer pressure," Tusker said and fished a cigarette out, then lit it from Carl's lighter, a battered Zippo knockoff, branded with the logo of the Pickwick restaurant in Duluth, Minnesota.

"Uh huh," Carl muttered and blew out a stream of smoke into the crisp October night. "I bet it's that therapist. She's the one who got you wrenching on your old man's truck."

Carl wasn't a man of many words or particularly deep philosophical ruminations, but he had an uncanny knack for reading Tusker, and a laser-like way of cutting to a point. They'd been friends since high school, a camaraderie born out of shared awkwardness and forged over countless bowls of afternoon cereal and high-minded pop music lyrics. At the time, Tusker didn't know that Carl's dad was abusive or that he'd go right to the toilet and put his finger down his throat after all those bowls of cereal.

They'd drifted apart for a few years but found each other again in adulthood, with a new shared passion— diving shipwrecks. Every weekend for a few years they were out diving any old pile of lumber on the lakebed. Tusker let Carl tag along on boat dives on the deeper stuff, while he was racking up bottom time pursuing his PhD in archaeology. They didn't dive together much anymore, sometimes not even once a season on the Great Lakes. But they still tried to meet up for a beer now and then and helped each other out with odd projects.

In his forties now, Carl had taken on a decidedly weathered look, probably from too many cigarettes and a bit too much beer. He'd put on some weight and gotten a little jowly, with a dirty mustache and thinning hair he kept stuffed under the same faded beanie with the logo of the shipyard where he worked as an engineer. But his grey-blue eyes were still clear and piercing, and his humor equally so. Carl was also a damn good mechanic, which would come in handy getting the Scout running again. Or so Tusker hoped.

Tusker sucked on the cigarette and gazed across at the glow of light emanating from inside the cabin. He could hear the waves lapping against the dock beyond and made a mental note to get the dock out of the water before the lake started to ice over. Yet another thing his father had drilled into him.

"Yeah, Dr. Fuchs told me to go through Dad's stuff. Seemed to think it might help me come to terms with some of the stuff I'm dealing with from Sri Lanka," Tusker finally replied. "She called that my 'war' and I didn't buy it, but I figure it's worth it to keep an open mind."

"Hey, you won't get any argument from me," Carl said. Both of them were looking into the distance, not at each other. "Therapy pretty much saved my ass after everything I went through. Not that it helped me get closer to my dad, but that wasn't really the point."

"Good thing we had our moms, eh?" Tusker chuckled, then stubbed out his cigarette on the side of the shed door. They turned to go back inside.

Two hours later, Carl had rebuilt the Scout's ignition system, replacing the electronic system with an old condenser and points they found in a dusty box labeled "Scout Parts" on a shelf at the back of the shed. "Less sophisticated, but more reliable," Carl said.

"Just like you," Tusker said with a wink as he cleaned off and reinstalled the spark plugs and reconnected the air intake to the carburetor.

Carl smirked. "Alright, if this doesn't work, I give up." Tusker knew Carl would never give up, but didn't say so. He climbed behind the wheel, pulled the choke lever wide open, wiggled the shifter to make sure it was in neutral, pumped the gas pedal a few times and turned the ignition key. The Scout roared to life with a cough and a cloud of black smoke from the exhaust. Carl howled and did a victory dance. Tusker revved the engine until the exhaust cleared and the truck settled into a loping but steady idle. The perfume of old car exhaust filled the shed, and it wasn't long before the nostalgia of the smell gave way to nausea. Tusker shut off the ignition and ran out of the hazy shed, seeking fresh air.

Carl followed, with two bottles of beer he'd gotten from a cooler, and he passed one to Tusker and popped the top on his own. "Here's to old trucks." They clinked bottles and drank. "The old Tusk Scout rides again. You're going to need to get those license plates renewed. When were they last legal — 1977?"

"'78," Tusker replied. "The year Dad got the bends."

"Right," Carl said, taking a pull on his bottle. "What a pity we were never old enough to appreciate that truck. Did you ever even ride in it?"

"I was just a toddler," Tusker said. "And when I was older, Dad just had me maintaining it for him, as if one day he'd drive it again."

"Or maybe he wanted you to drive it one day," Carl looked over at Tusker. "And now here you are. I can't wait to see that old thing on the road again."

"You ever think of becoming a therapist?" Tusker laughed. "You have a knack for it."

"Ha," Carl said. "Maybe so. You know they always say that the most screwed up people end up becoming therapists." He finished his beer and checked his watch. It was the same old Citizen Aqualand dive watch he'd worn as long as Tusker could remember. The timing ring was long gone and the rubber strap was faded to a dull gray. "Hey, it's late," he said. "I gotta go. Guessing you won't mind cleaning up?"

"I can manage," Tusker replied. "Thanks for the help." Carl slipped out of his coveralls and stuffed them in the backseat of his battered Subaru, then pulled on a blue down jacket festooned with duct tape over its many rips.

"I expect to be picked up in that thing next time I see you," Carl said, pointing towards the Scout as he started his car. Tusker nodded and waved. The headlamp beams arced away from him and the red taillights disappeared up the gravel driveway. He heard the Subaru's boxer engine rev as Carl drove off.

Back in the shed, there was still the distinct smell of gasoline and exhaust, so Tusker left the big swinging doors open as he put tools away in drawers and on the pegboard above the workbench. It was too quiet now that he was alone. He clicked on the old transistor radio, the only one he ever remembered in the shed. It was a Panasonic, spattered with paint, hung on a hook below the fluorescent light fixture.

"Next week marks the anniversary of the death of Senator Clay Overbrook in a plane crash in 1978," the woman reporter said. "And to mark the occasion, Senator Ted Hockenheimer will be making an appearance in Marquette to dedicate a memorial statue at Lakeside Park. For Hockenheimer, the frontrunner in next month's presidential campaign, the appearance is also a campaign stop in his late rival's old hometown..."

Tusker paused and listened, thinking back to last week on the *Keweenaw*, seeing the plane wreck on sonar, and what Sarah had said about her grandfather, and how it couldn't have been pilot error.

"This could be an awkward occasion for Hockenheimer, as he directly benefitted from Overbrook's death and has retained his Senate seat ever since. There are also questions about his controversial stance on the proposed trade deal with Russia,

as well as the pipeline under the Mackinaw Straits, which he supports. Michigan is a battleground state this year and Hockenheimer will no doubt face some difficult questions here next week. For Michigan Public Radio, this is Leila Mansour reporting from Marquette."

That's where he recognized the name! Tusker remembered the e-mail from Leila Mansour. She'd even sent a follow-up e-mail saying she'd be in Marquette for the dedication event. *I can drive over for it and meet her there,* Tusker thought. *What's the harm?* The radio station switched over to its overnight BBC World Service broadcast and Tusker put the dismantled electronic ignition parts from the Scout back in the parts box. He slid it onto the shelf, where he figured it would remain untouched for another thirty years.

Next to it was a green, dented ammunition box, the kind used to transport M60 machine gun cartridges. He'd always liked the castoff military paraphernalia his father kept around the house and cabin—old canvas tarps that smelled of the woods, a gas mask still in its carry bag, a rubber Aquala dive suit. He pulled the box off the shelf and set it on the workbench. The lid opened with some protest, revealing a jumble of old papers, a couple of scratched cassette tape boxes, and a wad of photographs. He shut the box and tucked it under his arm, clicked off the radio and fluorescent light, and shut the shed doors. It was a good night with Carl. They didn't really do heart to heart talks, but their best times together were spent doing things—diving wrecks, fixing a roof, wrenching on the Scout.

Tusker carried the ammunition box into the cabin. It had

gotten cold outside, and it reminded him that winter wouldn't be far off now, and he still had a lot to do to get ready: taking in the dock, splitting firewood, taking screens off the windows. He hadn't built a fire and the cabin was cold. He set the box on the small dining table and switched on the space heater under the window. It banged and popped as it warmed up and gave off a vague burning smell he remembered from childhood.

He pulled the leftover container of couscous from the fridge and proceeded to consume its contents in about three bites. Should he have offered Carl dinner? When Tusker got going on a project, he often forgot to take breaks or eat. He tossed the empty container in the recycle bin and sat down at the table with the ammunition box. He glanced at his watch. It was late, very late. But he was still a little wired from working on the truck and Dr. Fuchs had suggested he revisit Dad's mementos. The Scout was a start. Just half an hour, then sleep... He opened the hinged lid of the box.

Letters from Dad to Mom, and Mom to Dad. *Save those for another time.* It felt oddly intrusive to read those anyway. There was his Navy diving certificate, a logbook, his Silver Star medal, awarded for saving that downed pilot offshore from Nha Trang. What was that doing almost discarded in the back of the shed? There were photos, some black and white, some in faded Kodachrome, many stained and spilled on. He squinted at one. It showed two men standing on the deck of a boat, dressed only in olive green swim trunks. They both wore enormous wristwatches. Dive cylinders with accordion style regulator hoses lay on the deck beside them, and they both had wide grins on their faces. Between them, they held up a huge fish, a barracuda by the looks of it. The man on the right was Black. It was Chester Basch. The other man was Tusker's father. He flipped the photograph over. On the back was written in sloppy ballpoint ink: "*Gone fishing. Mekong Delta, April, '69*".

Tusker propped the photo up against a hurricane lamp in the middle of the table and smiled. *Dad was happy once,* he thought. In the back of the box, and clearly what had made it so heavy, was a bulky black object. He fished it out. It was a camera, a Nikonos, the old underwater film type. Tusker remembered his dad having several around the house, and he used to let him play with them. Tusker had enjoyed the weight of them, the tactile pleasure of pushing the big orange shutter release button, flicking the spring-loaded film advance lever, and playing with the knobs to adjust focus.

Maybe I'll buy a roll of film and resurrect this dinosaur, he thought. On the side of the camera there was a locking clamp, and he twisted the release. The back cover snapped open, and he hinged it back, expecting to see the empty take-up sprocket.

Shit! He slammed the lid shut and locked it. There was a roll of film in it. He'd probably ruined it by exposing it to light, at least the last few frames. He wondered what was on the roll. It was like finding sunken treasure, and he cursed his own carelessness for not checking whether it contained a roll of film before opening it. *It's late. I'm in no state to be fiddling with this now. Carl still shoots film. He'll know how to salvage the roll.*

He set the camera aside. It lay there, black and heavy and inanimate, a talisman from his father's mysterious past, yet the roll of film somehow alive inside, full of hidden secrets and potential. He switched off the light, laid down on the sofa and fell asleep to the sounds of the dark waves lapping the shore outside.

Red Diver, Blue Diver

Monroe, North Carolina.
March, 1966.

In late March of 1966, the James Bond film *Thunderball* had a run of showings at the Plaza Theater in Monroe, North Carolina. In the movie, a NATO bomber is hijacked and sunk in the waters off the Bahamas in order to steal its nuclear warheads. Bond does underwater battle with the villain and his aquatic henchmen, dodging sharks and spearguns before he saves the day. The plot was about as exotic and foreign to a 1960s audience in the small southern town of Monroe as one could get, especially to a young Black teenager, Chester Basch. But it captured his imagination and changed his life.

Chester was sixteen when he saw *Thunderball* at the Plaza. The theater was segregated back then, with the Black audience consigned to the so-called "Buzzards' Roost" of the hot and crowded upper balcony, and Chester was forced to watch the movie from behind a column, craning his neck as he competed for a partial view with others.

The diving scenes captivated Chester—the way Bond and the girl, Domino, were able to kick effortlessly among the coral, and the excitement when 007 penetrated the sunken airplane and found the dead hijacker in the pilot's seat. He was struck by two things. First, there were no Black people in the movie, but second, that underwater, it didn't seem to make a difference. Everybody was vulnerable there, living on borrowed time, no matter who they were. Diving seemed like a great equalizer. Chester walked out of *Thunderball* knowing what he wanted to do with his life.

The United States had been formally at war with North Vietnam for less than three years when Chester Basch got off a Greyhound bus and walked into the Great Lakes Naval Training Station. It was there that he met Jonathan Tusk, a Michigander who'd enlisted only a month earlier. Tusk gave Chester the nickname, "Basher,"and the two struck up a friendship, strengthened by their mutual ambition to become Navy Divers, with the ultimate goal of joining the Underwater Demolition Team. They were lucky in that the war created a huge need for qualified divers and the UDT was actively seeking new candidates.

Before they could even get a shot at the UDT, Tusk and Basch had to learn to dive in all the Navy's disciplines—open circuit scuba, closed circuit rebreather, and surface-supplied hard hat diving. They did their training in the murky, cold waters of Lake Michigan, practicing navigation, emergency ascents, surveying, hull inspection, even underwater combat. After six months of intensive training, Tusk and Basch finished one and two in their class and were sent to Coronado, California, home of Underwater Demolition Team 11.

Becoming a UDT diver was incredibly difficult and the

success rate for candidates abysmally low, but Tusk and Basch trained hard, pushing each other, running miles after dark, swimming extra laps, competing with each other in pushups. Their hard work paid off and both flew to Saigon in early 1968, newly minted frogmen. What they did, and what they saw, during their years of deployment in Vietnam, would affect them in ways no one else could truly relate to, and that only each other could understand. When they left the UDT in 1970, Tusk went on to support the Department of the Interior's joint Tektite II project with NASA, while Basch became an instructor back at Great Lakes. Six years later, they were diving together again, as part of the Mobile Diving and Salvage Unit, diving the wreck of a crashed plane in Lake Superior. For Basher, it was full circle, he thought at the time. His own "Operation Thunderball."

Early December, 1978, Lake Superior.

The United States Coast Guard Cutter *Sundew* was fighting to hold her position on a three-point mooring. The crew had seen its share of winter weather on the Great Lakes, but supporting a salvage operation in January was an entirely new challenge. Conditions were deemed too rough for a support barge, so the Navy's Mobile Diving and Salvage Unit decided to try deploying divers directly off the 180-foot cutter, using a deck deco chamber and winch-lowered stage. Ice floes, ten-foot swells, and the cold were making things dangerously difficult.

A northwest gale was blowing waves across the *Sundew's* bow, freezing into impressive ice sculptures on the foredeck equipment. Support crew were being rotated every thirty minutes to avoid hypothermia. And when one compressor began to freeze up, losing precious daylight hours, hot air blowers were flown over by helicopter to be deployed on deck. Everyone on board could tell the window of opportunity to salvage the sunken airliner was closing.

190 feet below, two divers, Petty Officer First Class Jonathan Tusk and his buddy, Petty Officer Second Class Chester Basch, were struggling to maintain their footing on the muddy lake bed. Visibility was arm's length at best, and the thick bundles of taped umbilical cables and hoses that connected them to the *Sundew* were going from taut to slack with the huge winter swells, tugging at the men so that they bounced up and down, releasing plumes of silt.

Tusk wanted to signal his frustration to Basch, but he couldn't see his partner through the billowing cloud. He was also very cold. He squinted at the tiny thermometer clipped to the strap of his Aquastar watch. It read somewhere below 35 degrees Fahrenheit. His DUI Hot Water Suit was barely lukewarm, and he was beginning to shiver uncontrollably.

"Hot water line is kinked!" Tusk shouted into his helmet mic. "I'm freezing my balls off down here!"

"Say again, Red Diver," the reply from Lowry, *Sundew's* dive supervisor, came back. His voice was tinny and garbled. The cold did strange things to electronics. Things were already not going well. Tusk decided to just get on with it.

The divers had two objectives: locating the bodies of any passengers still trapped in the passenger cabin, and determining what had caused the plane to wind up at the bottom of the lake. It quickly occurred to Tusk that both of these would likely be impossible in the current conditions.

The three disembodied sections of the wrecked Gulfstream II were all lying upright and close together, but nearly half sunk in the soft mud. The divers were armed with pry bars and torches. Tusk had also clipped to his harness a heavy, black Nikonos IV-A, Nikon's latest underwater camera. Though it wasn't available publicly yet, the Navy had negotiated with the Japanese camera maker to provide prototypes for its underwater survey work. Its revolutionary new automatic exposure function was a leap forward in underwater photography. The camera was mounted on an aluminum bracket with an articulating arm that held an SB-105 strobe, but Tusk knew the flash would be no match for the darkness he now faced.

"Basher, you seeing anything?" Tusk said into his helmet comms through chattering teeth.

"Only by braille, my man," he replied in his distinctly Southern accent. Basch was from rural North Carolina, a sharecropper's son who'd gone on to become the Navy's first Black diver to be awarded a Silver Star. There was no one Jonathan Tusk trusted more underwater.

"Getting bodies out is gonna be impossible in these conditions," Tusk grunted through labored breathing. "Let's get on with the survey. See what we can find."

"Uh huh," Basch replied. "Let's start at the tail and move forward."

The men crept along, arms out, sweeping their torches back and forth. Tusk's light caught a reflection. "Got a window," he said, matter-of-factly. He let the torch fall on its tether at his waist and braced himself against the bulk of the plane. Suddenly, he was yanked upwards, then slammed back against the fuselage, narrowly missing a direct impact on his helmet.

"Slack!" he shouted into his helmet mic and gave his tether two short, hard tugs. "Topside, I need some slack down here, goddammit! This almost makes me miss 'Nam."

"Was a helluva lot warmer, I'll give it that," Basch replied. "I see you now. I'm comin' over." The two divers stood on the mud a few feet apart. Tusk could see Basch's huge bulk inside his orange suit and his reassuring face through the rectangular faceplate of his Morse Mk 12 helmet. Basch turned and looked towards the plane; its ghostly shape came and went as if through a fog. But something was not right.

"Reports were that she came down nose first, right?" Basch said.

"Yup," Tusk replied.

"Then why is the tail missing?" Basch said, pointing his prybar at the void. Tusk strained his eyes and looked. The shape of the plane came into better focus. He crept forward. Sure enough, the entire rear stabilizer was gone, as if sheared off. Immediately it reminded Tusk of the downed Air Force jets he'd seen in the Mekong Delta.

"I'm going to climb up and have a closer look," he said. The next time the *Sundew* rode the crest of a swell, the divers were pulled off the lakebed and Tusk timed a jump perfectly, alighting on the rounded top of the crumpled fuselage. He crept back on all fours, almost riding the plane like a horse. Then it just ended in space. Tusk looked down at the gaping wound. Both engine were completely missing as was the entire rear of the plane.

He raised the Nikonos to his faceplate and peered through its tiny viewfinder. This would be pure guesswork. He flipped the camera upside down and studied the markings on front of the 35-millimeter lens, dialed the aperture open to f/2.5 and set the focus to infinity. *As much light as possible and pray enough would get in focus.* He powered on the strobe and heard its capacitor's high-pitched whine as it boosted voltage. Then he aimed at the scene below him and started shooting. He prayed that in this cold water, the camera and strobe batteries would last the full twenty-four exposures on the roll of Agfa 800 film a crew member had loaded on the *Sundew*.

After firing a few frames, Tusk paused and examined the wreck some more. He could just make out a few rows of seats, a collapsed rear bulkhead, and a jumble of wiring and debris. According to the flight manifest, all of the passengers had been seated in the first few rows of the cabin, so the seats in this aft section were empty. No bodies to recover here. He leaned closer, so that his faceplate was a foot from the jagged edge of the fuselage. It was blackened, as if it was subjected to intense heat. Had the engine caught fire? This was clearly the cause of the crash. They were lucky to find it so early. But where were the two missing engines now? He readjusted the focus distance on the Nikonos and shot five more frames with numb fingers.

"Topside, did sonar show any other debris field away from the plane? Over," he called up to the *Sundew* on his helmet comms.

After a long pause, a response came down. "Negative, Red Diver. Nothing else nearby. Over."

"The entire back of the plane is missing," he replied. "The tail and two engines are *somewhere*."

"Copy that, Red Diver," Lowry replied. "Shoot a few more photos, then get to the stage. Things are getting rather... nautical up here. We're gonna pull the plug. Over." The stage was a caged aluminum platform, winched from the ship, on which the divers rode to and from the lakebed. On the way up, they would pause for decompression stops before being transferred to the chamber on the *Sundew's* deck.

"Topside, just a few more minutes here. I'd like to have a closer look at this tail section. Over." Tusk said, clamoring down off the fuselage, scrabbling for purchase on the slippery aluminum.

"Both divers—travel in FIVE," came the stern reply. "Get to the stage. Over." Tusk didn't say anything. Basch was waiting for him on the lakebed. Tusk gestured to him. They both bounded in low gravity strides around to the back of the plane. Tusk made a sweeping circular motion with his arm without saying anything into his helmet comms. Basch gave him an OK sign to show he understood. They fanned out walking in an arc opposite each other, casting their torches back and forth, up and down.

"Jonny, over here," Basch said after a minute. Tusk bounced over. In the beam of Basch's torch was a cylinder, about the length of a garden rake, its diameter slightly fatter. It was embedded in the side of what was left of the fuselage. At the end that stuck out were four twisted pieces of metal. Fins, Tusk thought, and a chill went through him that wasn't from the cold water. *No wonder this wrecked plane looked like the ones in Vietnam*. He looked over at Basch. He'd seen it too. Neither of them said anything, but Tusk advanced the film and fired off frame after frame until the film advance lever jammed, indicating the end of the roll.

"Both divers—square yourselves away, return to the stage and standby to travel. Things are rough. Over."

The divers made their way in the general direction of the stage, which hovered ten feet off the lakebed, though they couldn't see it through the silt-induced gloaming. The plane was swallowed up by the same cloud behind them, leaving them in a sort of half-lit no man's land between the wreck site and their way back to safety.

An hour in the cold had brought on full blown hypothermia and Tusk was shivering uncontrollably now. He was dreaming of the overheated humidity of the cramped deco chamber on board the *Sundew*. But first, an hour of decompression, on the swaying platform in the depths of the icy lake. He hoped he had gotten at least a few decent photos, which no doubt the Navy brass and NTSB would analyze with great interest.

"Both divers, big swells up here, guys," came Lowry's voice in their helmets. "Hang on. Over."

Tusk looked over at Basch, who nodded and made an exaggerated "you first" gesture. Tusk clipped the Nikonos to his harness and pulled, hand over hand, on his umbilical, which snaked up into the darkness, twisted through a stanchion of the stage as a precaution. He could see the stage suspended above him. Just as he reached the underside of the swaying platform, the *Sundew* was hit by a 12-foot wave, causing it to ride high over the crest and slam down into the trough. The stage was pulled up, then fell like an elevator with its cable cut. The heavy platform caught Tusk squarely on top of his helmet. Then all went black.

Chester Basch saw it happen, ten feet below on the lakebed. Jonathan Tusk fell, as if in slow motion, from below the stage, landing in a crumpled heap on the lakebed, sending up a plume of silt.

"Topside, we have an emergency down here. Red Diver is down!" Basch shouted into his helmet comms and shuffled over to where his longtime partner lay motionless.

"Blue Diver, can he make it back to the stage? Over."

"No, damn it, topside, he's out. I repeat, Red Diver is out." Basch put his arms under Tusk's and pulled him to a sitting position in the mud. It was difficult to work in the near whiteout and the sticky ankle-deep mud. He peered into Tusk's faceplate. He could see a dark liquid around the seal of the acrylic, emanating from somewhere on the top of Tusk's head.

"He's bleeding and unconscious. Head wound," Basch spoke matter of factly, switching into a sort of mechanical action mode. *UDT doesn't leave anyone behind, he thought. Come on, Jonny.*

"Blue Diver, we need Red Diver to complete his in-water deco if at all possible before we pull him. Over." Navy standard procedure for an unconscious diver weighed the risk of almost certain decompression sickness against his injuries, with the bends usually deemed more serious. Staying on the stage for deco was usually recommended.

"Screw protocol," Basch said. "He won't make it on the stage for an hour. I need you to lower the stage to the bottom so I can get him on," he panted.

"Affirmative, Blue Diver. We'll need you to stay on the bottom and then complete your deco after we offload Red Diver into the chamber up here. Over."

The stage landed on the mud nearby, rocking back and forth from the tension on the winch cable and the pitching ship 190 feet above. Basch dragged Tusk, step by step, to the stage, then heaved his dead weight onto the platform. As a precaution, he clipped Tusk to the steel mesh with a snap ring.

"OK, topside, pull him up," Basch gasped. "Just don't forget me down here." He would have to wait for his elevator ride back to the surface until they'd offloaded Tusk for emergency treatment inside the deco chamber.

"Traveling," came the reply from above, and the platform, with Tusk's limp form, disappeared into the grey light above, swallowed by a cloud of silt. Chester Basch never felt so alone.

Basher

Munising, Michigan.
Present day.

"Uncle Chester?" Tusker knocked lightly on the door and stepped cautiously into the room. Chester Basch was sitting in a recliner with his back to the door, gazing out the window at a squirrel raiding a bird feeder. There was an oxygen tank in a rack next to him, a rubber hose snaking over his shoulder.

"Damn rodents," he said without looking back. "Who's asking?"

"It's Julian," Tusker said. "Julian Tusk."

Chester swiveled his upper body and looked, his eyes wide. Then his face broke into a broad grin. "I'll be damned," he called, "Jonny's boy. I haven't seen you in, how long?"

"Gotta be over twenty years," Tusker said. It was closer to thirty. Chester had come by the cabin with a box of Tusker's dad's stuff a month after the funeral. Tusker remembers his mother crying on the porch as she and Chester talked, and how Chester told him he'd take

Tusker diving one day when he was older. But he never saw him again.

"What brings you by, Jules?" Tusker had forgotten Chester used to call him that, and he hated it. He forced a smile. He looked around the room. It was the typically bland decor of elderly care facilities, where individualizing was inefficient when residents rotated through so regularly. The walls were an inoffensive shade of beige and the sparse furniture looked leftover from the 1980s—wood veneer finished in a shade called something like "Early American" or "Honey Walnut." At least the artwork vaguely reflected Chester's life at sea: a reproduction of Winslow Homer's *Boys in a Boat* hung over the bed.

Tusker pulled the lone empty chair over so that he could face Chester. "I was passing by and heard you were living here now," he lied. He'd had to make a few phone calls to track down Chester. As it turned out, his ex-wife still kept the name Basch, and told Tusker that Chester had moved into the Our Lady of Comfort Care Home in Munising.

Chester eyed him suspiciously. "Lydia told you, didn't she?" He reached up to adjust the nosepiece of his oxygen tube. Tusker saw the old Tudor dive watch hanging loosely on his once muscular wrist.

"I'm that bad a liar, huh?" Tusker laughed. "Actually, I was going through some of Dad's old things the other night and came across some photos I thought you might like to see." He reached into his faded canvas shoulder bag and pulled out a large envelope. He opened the flap and extracted the small pile of photographs, handing them to Chester. The old diver's hands shook badly, and he dropped the photos on the carpeting. They fanned out in an unruly pile.

"Goddamn hands," he cursed. "Don't work like they used to." Tusker bent and gathered them up and set the pile on a side table, shifting aside a clutter of prescription pill bottles and a copy of the day's newspaper. He saw Senator Hockenheimer's photo on the front page.

"Don't worry, I've got you," Tusker said, and handed Chester the photos one by one.

"Ah, that big old 'cuda," he said, examining the picture of him and Jonathan Tusk with the big fish. "We were waiting to assist in an exfil offshore from the mouth of the Red River, and this barracuda kept swimming circles around us. Your dad got a little nervous, so he finally baited it with a hot dog on a gaff and when it came close, he stabbed the son of a bitch with that big knife he used to carry. I don't think he was prepared for how that fish would fight." Chester laughed until he coughed violently.

"You OK? Want some water?" Tusker scanned the room for a water bottle.

"It's this damn emphysema," Chester said, catching his breath. "Never thought I'd be breathing off a cylinder again, but here I am." He gestured at the oxygen tank. "Anyway, we had a good old fish fry that night, right there on the poop deck of the *Long Beach*."

Tusker smiled and proceeded to hand him the other

photos, one by one, and spent the next half hour listening to Chester recount stories for each picture. Finally, he collected them all and slid the pile back into the envelope.

"What do you remember about the crash?" he finally said, clearing his throat.

Chester shifted uneasily in the recliner and looked back out at the birdfeeder. The squirrel was gone and a pair of cardinals now picked at the sunflower seeds.

"You working with that journalist?" He eyed Tusker suspiciously.

"What journalist?" Tusker pretended he didn't know about Leila Mansour.

"That Arab lady."

"No, I just got curious…" Tusker replied.

Chester waited a long time before speaking, and then did so with a hushed, sober voice.

"The Navy did wrong by your father after that dive," he said, bitterly. "We never should have been out there in those conditions to begin with, and then they pulled the plug on it and yanked us up. It was careless, and then they made sure he didn't talk about it afterwards."

"Talk about what?" Tusker leaned in and asked.

Chester looked over Tusker's shoulder towards the door,

conspiratorially. "About what we found down there," he said. "They ruled the cause of that crash was 'pilot error' but that's bullshit."

"What was the cause, do you think?"

"Something was just not right with that plane," Chester shook his head. "The nose was crumpled, but then the whole tail was missing!" His eyes widened and searched Tusker's face.

"I found Dad's old Nikonos at the cabin. Still has a roll of film in it..."

"You'd best leave all this alone, Jules," Chester interrupted him. "That film doesn't exist, you hear me?"

"I just need to get the roll processed," Tusker said.

"It. Doesn't. Exist." Chester enunciated each word, then broke into another coughing spell, this one longer and more violent than the last. A nurse came in, hurrying over to Chester. Tusker stepped away to make room for her and watched as she removed his tube and placed a breathing mask over his nose and mouth, strapping it on the back of his head. She turned up the dial on a nebulizer and Tusker saw the mask fill with moisture. Chester's breathing was labored.

"You'd better go," the nurse said to Tusker. Her tone suggested it was not up for negotiation. Tusker leaned in to Chester and laid a hand on his shoulder.

"So long, Uncle Chester," he said. "I'll stop by again, maybe next week." Chester didn't respond. Tusker picked up his bag and walked out of the room, looking back to see Chester leaning back in his chair, the old diver struggling to catch his breath.

Senator Hockenheimer

Marquette, Michigan.
Present day.

Lakeside Park was a circus. Normally, a late October morning would find the park empty, save for a few hardy joggers or fishermen casting off the boardwalk. A raw wind blew in across the water leaving no doubt that autumn was over. Any remaining leaves on the maples that lined Lakeshore Boulevard had long been shaken loose and were swirling among the parked cars and media trucks that now jockeyed for nearby parking spots. Reporters, camera operators, a small crowd of protesters and a larger one of supporters huddled, waiting for the arrival of Senator Ted Hockenheimer. He was late.

Tusker had decided to make Marquette the destination for the maiden voyage of the resurrected Scout. After a slow and noisy two-hour drive on the winding back roads, his legs were stiff and his back sore. Parking downtown was a mess on the best of days, so he opted to park in the Maritime Museum's lot and walk back to stretch his legs. He pulled his watch cap down over his ears and buttoned the neck flap on his Barbour jacket. When the clouds started spitting a cold rain, he smiled smugly. He'd finally gotten around to waxing the cotton and the water beaded up on his shoulders.

He arrived at Lakeside Park just in time to see a black Chevy Suburban glide to a dramatic stop. A tall woman with broad shoulders and close-cropped hair stepped out of the passenger door. She was dressed in a snugly fitting black Kevlar jacket and pants. Aside from her decidedly tactical getup and athletic build, she stood out in the largely white northern Michigan crowd because she was African American. She also wore dark glasses despite the overcast day, lending her a look of menace as she took in the scene. Tusker could see a coiled earpiece trailing down inside her collar. She slowly scanned from side to side, no doubt identifying possible threats, before opening the rear door of the SUV.

Senator Ted Hockenheimer emerged, a well-practiced grin already on his face. The senator squinted into the wind, smoothed his impressive head of silver hair, and waved to the gathered crowd. He was tall and, despite being well into his seventies, still bore the upright posture of the military man he once was. His image was one of fitness and virility, and he played it up by often holding press conferences after workouts, sweating in a tracksuit. Today he wore a dark blazer and red tie under a long wool overcoat.

The woman, who Tusker assumed was his bodyguard, stepped out in front of him, creating a tunnel in the throng of people reaching out with smartphones, signs and big cameras. The senator followed her forward onto the grass, and they strode across it to the circle of new bricks that surrounded a draped sculpture, where he joined Marquette's mayor, the city's police chief, and a couple of other local dignitaries Tusker didn't recognize. They were talking quietly to each other while the crowd began to close in, forming a ring around the group.

The bodyguard eyed the crowd, one hand perched near the zipper of her jacket, the other touching her earpiece. She said something into the collar of her jacket and a moment later, a staff member appeared carrying an umbrella, which he deployed and held dutifully over the senator's head against the drizzle. At the back of the crowd, Tusker could read a few signs some of the protesters held up. In messy handwriting that was starting to run from the rain, one said, "Blood on Your Hands." Another one read, "Oil and Water Don't Mix." A third: "Don't Hock US to Russia." Senator Hockenheimer couldn't have missed them, but he pretended they weren't there as he began his speech.

"I'm so grateful for the warm welcome to Marquette on such a cold day," he said into a microphone on the lectern that had been wheeled onto the plaza moments before. "But we're Michiganders, and a little rain and wind doesn't bother us, does it?" There was a smattering of applause. *Hockenheimer was born in New Jersey,* Tusker thought. The senator nodded in the direction of a few people in the front row and scanned the crowd, careful to avert his eyes from the protestors.

"Now I know there's the small matter of a presidential election coming up in a couple of weeks, and I encourage all of you to get out there and vote like your lives depend on it. Well, except you folks holding the signs back there.

You can stay home." He smiled and laughed at his own joke, joined by many in the crowd.

"But I'm not here today to talk about politics or elections," he continued, his tone switching to a more serious tenor. "We're here today to honor the memory of a great American, and a former colleague of mine. Clay Overbrook may have been a rival, but we were also friends, and I valued his tenacity and the vigor he put into his work as a U.S. Senator. It inspired me to work even harder in my own career." More applause.

"It was a sad day back in 1978," he paused and cleared his throat. "It was a day similar to this one— cold, windy, close to an important election—when we lost Clay Overbrook, and I've missed him on the Hill every day since." The rain was steadier now. People were holding newspapers, jackets, and campaign flyers over their heads in a futile attempt to keep from getting soaked. Hockenheimer went on, dry under the big black umbrella.

"Senator Overbrook may have been on the other side of the aisle from me, but we stood for many of the same values, the values we as Michiganders believe in— freedom, justice, that hard work should be rewarded." Many were shuffling their feet now. It was starting to sound like a campaign speech after all, Tusker thought, and checked his watch. He started to tune the words out and looked out past the massive ore dock to the lake, where a low cloud deck cast an eerie aura.

"Now I don't want to go on too long here or we're going to all need a boat." *Finally*. "So without further ado, I'd like to bring Evelyn Overbrook up to help me unveil this memorial to her late husband—a friend, a patriot, and a great American, Senator Clay Overbrook."

The crowd clapped and hooted warmly as an elderly woman was helped up from a folding chair in the front row and shuffled forward. Tusker remembered Evelyn Overbrook from years earlier. She had taken up the activism of her late husband after his death, and even launched an exploratory campaign to run for his old seat against Hockenheimer in the 1980s. But now she was a stooped old woman, resigned to playing second fiddle again to the senator.

She gave Ted Hockenheimer a cursory, small smile and shook his hand. He handed her a tassled gold cord and stepped back. The mayor nodded to her, urging her to pull, and she did. The heavy cloth on the 15-foot-tall statue slid down off of Clay Overbrook's bronze head. The crowd applauded. The cloth got snagged on the statue's outstretched arm, which pointed out to the lake, in the direction where Overbrook had died. An aide rushed forward and freed it and it fell away. It was a reasonable likeness, Tusker thought, based on photos he'd seen of Overbrook.

Afterward, the crowd began to disperse, some moving around the senator, others making for their cars. The protesters began to chant something. Reporters converged on Hockenheimer's entourage. Tusker scanned the group for Leila Mansour. It was hard to make out faces now; everyone was hidden inside rain jackets or under umbrellas. He'd looked her up on the internet so he'd know who to look for—a striking woman with jet black short hair, a pierced aquiline nose, big brown eyes and thick black eyebrows. In fact, her parents were immigrants from Lebanon who'd traded Beirut for suburban Detroit during their home country's violence in the 1980s.

Suddenly there was a commotion. A protester, a smaller woman in a red foul weather shell, approached Hockenheimer and was shouting at him. Tusker watched as the towering bodyguard physically lifted the protester off her feet and threw her several feet back so she landed, skidding, on the wet grass. Tusker ran over to see if the woman was alright. She sat up and pulled her hood back from her face, grimacing in pain.

"Sarah?" Tusker said, surprised. It was Sarah, his PhD student, whose grandfather had been the pilot on Overbrook's plane. "Are you alright?" He squatted next to her.

"I'm fine, thanks, Dr. Tusk," she said. "Typical strongarm response from Hockenheimer and his henchmen."

"Henchwoman," Tusker corrected her and glanced over his shoulder at the bodyguard, who glowered at them from across the plaza now. No one else seemed to have noticed the incident. "Are you OK to get up?" Tusker extended a hand. Sarah took it and stood gingerly.

"More of a bruised ego than anything," Sarah replied. "That crook has a lot to answer for, and my list of complaints just got longer."

Tusker smiled. "I didn't realize you were such an activist," he said.

"It's not really activism. It's citizenship. And more people need to wake up to that fact." She brushed dirt off her wet jeans and picked up her crumpled sign. "Anyway, we made our point and, I guess, in the end, this day should be more for Mrs. Overbrook than that jackass." She gestured towards the senator, who was speaking to a group of journalists, his face illuminated by bright video lights.

"Thanks for your help, Dr. Tusk," Sarah said. "I should get going. I owe you a paper next week." She smiled. "Oh, I never asked why you're here today. Tell me you're not a Hockenheimer supporter!"

Tusker was tempted to tell her about his father's involvement in the plane crash investigation, his visit with Chester, the film he'd found. But instead, he just said, "I was just in town and curious what the action was." He smiled. Sarah waved as she limped away into the rain.

Tusker walked over to the back of the scrum of journalists surrounding Hockenheimer. He listened to the talking points the senator recited in response to every pointed question, no doubt rehearsed with his campaign staff.

"Senator, what about the rumors of Russian influence in the election?" There she was. Leila Mansour. There was no mistaking her in the otherwise conservative group of journalists in their earth tone rain jackets. Leila was wearing a black leather motorcycle jacket, complete with padded elbows and shoulders and a tab collar—Belstaff or something. Silver nickel zippers glinted in the hot video lights. Her hair was buzzed to the scalp on half her head with a long asymmetric pile of black curls, glossy with the rain, that hung over one eye in a sort of Goth pixie cut. She kept tossing her head to flick it out of the way. In addition to her nose piercing, the one ear that was exposed was perforated with silver studs as well. She had on faded denim jeans that Tusker noticed fit her perfectly, and black Doc Marten boots, the tall ones that laced almost up to her knees. Over her shoulder was a stained canvas dispatch bag, and though she was not tall—maybe five foot-one in her boots—her presence seemed to command respect among the other reporters.

"What nonsense," Hockenheimer responded, chuckling. "My opponent has been feeding these vile allegations to the media for months, and you know what? There's not a scrap of evidence. I'm a patriotic American, and if you think I'd let myself be aided, in any way, by any foreign power, you're dead wrong." He turned away from Leila, but she wasn't finished.

"Oh, I'm not just talking about this election," she half smiled and tossed her hair again. "You've been dogged by these allegations since, well, Senator Overbrook died unexpectedly." She gestured towards the statue, as if it was a surprise witness.

"You can't possibly think…" Hockenheimer was visibly flustered now. A campaign staffer stepped closer to him and started to say something. The senator waved him off. "I resent your implication, Miss…"

"Mansour. Leila Mansour, *Detroit Free Press.*"

"Miss Mansour, that accident was tragic and ill timed, and the result of human error. I've always won my elections by my own merit, through hard work and integrity."

"But if you're elected, your stance on trade will clearly benefit Russia, and hurt the Great Lakes steel industry…"

"We've run out of time for further questions for today," the senator's staffer stepped in holding up his hands. A groan went up from the assembled press. Hockenheimer's face had turned red and he looked disoriented. The journalists started putting away their equipment, the video lights were extinguished, and the crowd dispersed. Tusker took the opportunity to slice through a gap in the bodies and approached the senator.

"It wasn't pilot error," he simply said.

Hockenheimer turned around. "Excuse me?"

"You said the plane crash was the result of human error, but I don't believe it was. At least not the pilot's." He locked eyes with the senator. The bodyguard stepped forward. She was at least Tusker's height with shoulders just as wide. Tusker eyed her warily. He'd seen how she reacted to Sarah earlier.

"And you are…?" the senator said.

"Julian Tusk, professor of underwater archaeology at Michigan Tech," he said, as if his credentials gave him any authority here.

"Tusk… any relation to a… *Jonathan Tusk*?" Hockenheimer said.

"Yes, he was my father."

"Ah, my condolences then. I heard he passed away several years ago. Dive accident, wasn't it? His name has crossed my desk before."

"Probably on the plane crash investigation report," Tusker replied. "Which is what eventually killed him, as it happens."

"Yes, and we served together, briefly, in Vietnam," Hockenheimer said, ignoring the comment. "If you've read the report he contributed to, you'll know that the conclusion was pilot error."

"I've recently come across some new evidence that suggests otherwise," Tusker said.

"What sort of evidence?" The senator tilted his head and squinted. He'd stepped close to Tusker so that Tusker could smell the sour coffee on his breath.

Tusker simply smiled. He actually had no evidence at all. "Of course, this really is of no concern to you, I'm sure. It's ancient history and has no bearing on your campaign." Tusker tried to soften his tone with a smile. The bodyguard looked as if she would break his neck at the mere suggestion from her boss.

"No, no, it doesn't, Mr. Tusk, and I'd suggest you don't go picking at old scabs. I don't think poor Mrs. Overbrook could bear opening up that case again." He gave a smirk. "Of course, if there's anything I can do to help in the matter, don't hesitate to reach out. I'm sure I can muster the facilities to examine any of this… new evidence."

"I'll be sure to let you know," Tusker replied coldly. Senator Hockenheimer turned away, shook some hands, and was whisked to his waiting Suburban on the curb. Tusker watched as they drove off and saw the bodyguard watching out the passenger side window, studying him like a predator. He felt a shiver pass down his spine. It wasn't from the wind and rain blowing in off the lake.

"Mr. Tusk," Leila Mansour's voice broke the silence. Everyone else had left the park except for the two of them. He hadn't seen her standing there. He turned towards her. "You never replied to my e-mails."

"Yes, I apologize," Tusker fumbled for words. "I was doing some fieldwork in Jamaica, then finishing up some sonar runs with a few students and…"

"Look, I get it," she said. "We're all busy. But judging by your little chat with the senator, we have some mutual interests here."

"Let's just say I've been compelled to revisit my family history recently and this came up."

"Compelled by what?" she asked. *Journalist*. Ask the right questions, he thought.

"I'd rather not say, other than it's been very illuminating so far."

"You went to see Chester Basch," she cut in.

"How…?"

"I went to Our Lady of—what is it—Comfort, and they told me he'd had a visitor. Not doing too well, old Chester. They wouldn't even let me see him."

"Honestly, I was hoping I'd run into you here so I could at least apologize for not replying to your messages," he said.

She smiled for the first time, a big wide grin that softened her otherwise more severe demeanor.

"What was it you wanted to talk to me about anyway?" he asked.

"Pretty much what you told the senator," she said, and flipped open her dispatch bag and started rummaging in it. The rain had stopped but was that… a snow flurry? "I'd like to know more about this evidence you mentioned. Or were you bluffing?"

"Well, I haven't had a chance to really dig into it yet but his reaction to what I said spoke volumes. I'm thinking I should get out there and maybe dive the plane wreck and see it for myself."

She whistled through her teeth and shook her head.

"You're crazy, man. It's one thing living next to this big lake, but diving in it? Nope, not for me."

Tusker laughed. "Well, it's sort of what I do."

"For your sins," she said. "Anyway, what do you hope to find, and why is this suddenly so important to you? You a conspiracy theorist or something?"

"Would you believe me if I said my therapist told me to do it?"

She laughed out loud. "You really should find yourself a new therapist."

"Know any?"

"I'm a good listener…"

There was an awkward silence that hung in the air between them. Then she fished out a long shemagh, the sort of traditional cotton scarf worn by Afghani herdsmen and adopted by Special Forces soldiers. She coiled it three times around her neck and tucked it inside the collar of her leather jacket. Then she pulled out a full-face motorcycle helmet. Tusker looked surprised.

"What, never seen a chick on a bike before?"

"Sure, but not in this weather.," he replied.

"I ride til the snow flies."

"And you thought I was crazy for diving in the lake. You'd better hurry." Tusker looked skyward. Leila extended her hand. Tusker grasped it. It was surprisingly warm, her grip firm.

"I'll be in touch, Mr. Tusk," she said with a smile. "And next time, please get back to me."

"Oh, I will, don't worry," he said. "And you can call me Tusker."

She pulled the helmet down over her curls and cinched the chin strap tight, then pulled on some black leather riding gloves, gave him a wave, and walked across the wet grass towards the street. In one fluid motion, she swung a leg over a Royal Enfield Continental GT with a flame red fuel tank and kicked it to life. The engine burbled, she checked over her shoulder for traffic and gunned the little café racer onto Lakeside Boulevard. He watched her turn up Main Street and disappear from sight.

The Darkroom

Marquette, Michigan.
Present day.

Even over the rumble of the Scout's idling V8, Tusker could hear the music. It was the unmistakable banshee wail of Chris Cornell singing "Fell on Black Days." Tusker switched off the engine and climbed out of the truck, slamming the door. Carl lived in the house he grew up in, which was so familiar to Tusker from countless afternoons after school. Now it was the smallest house on the block, the others having been renovated beyond recognition or simply knocked down and replaced with bigger ones that all looked alike. He smiled and wondered what these new neighbors thought of Carl's musical taste.

"So it's a Soundgarden day, huh?" Tusker shouted above the music as he came in through the back door. He set the six pack of Bell's Two Hearted Ale on the kitchen counter. Carl turned and smiled, then lifted the needle off the record. The house went silent.

"It's never not a Soundgarden day," he replied, "and Cornell always sounds better on vinyl, turned up to eleven."

"I'm sure your neighbors agree," Tusker said.

"Eh, they need a little shaking up," he said. "Besides, the guy next door offends me more with his Hockenheimer yard sign."

Tusker smiled and popped the caps off two beers, handing one to Carl. Carl took it and walked over to the window.

"How's she running?" he gestured to the Scout.

"So far, so good," Tusker said. "Drips a fair amount of gear oil, but I guess I'm not surprised. Anyway, that's what gravel driveways are for."

"Maybe this winter we pull the gearbox and change the shaft seals."

"Maybe," Tusker replied reluctantly. Car repair was a fun hobby for Carl, but for him it was only out of necessity. "I like to think the truck is just changing its own fluids continuously. I just have to add oil every now and then."

Carl scowled, then changed the subject. "So what's up with this camera you found?"

Tusker reached into his bag and pulled out the Nikonos. "Like an idiot I opened up the back without checking if it had a roll in it."

Carl clucked his tongue. "Digital photography's made you soft."

"Yeah, well, it's also made my work a hell of a lot easier."
"Well, with any luck you didn't ruin the entire roll," Carl said, taking the camera from Tusker.

He finished his beer and grabbed a second bottle before leading Tusker to the basement. Carl's house was like a museum. The walls were covered in framed newspaper clippings, old sepia toned photos of ships and nautical ephemera he'd dumpster-dived from the shipyard, or collected on wreck dives before that practice became frowned upon. Every horizontal surface held models of ships, old camera components, and dusty, out of print books.

The basement was a mess. There was dive gear heaped on some metal shelving and a washer and dryer were covered in laundry in an unknown state of cleanliness. A sour smell emanated from somewhere and Tusker wrinkled his nose as he stepped over a crate of yellowing magazines.

"I think something's died down here," Carl said, as if it needed some explanation, but showing no great concern. He stepped across a raised threshold into a smaller room and waited for Tusker to follow him, then shut the door behind them and clicked on a wall switch. The room was bathed in a dim, red glow. By contrast to the rest of the basement, the darkroom was tidy. Across the far wall were strung drying lines for negatives, with evenly spaced butterfly clips. A workbench was on one side of the room, holding enlargers, and on the opposite wall was a series of trays for developing mixes. Shelves and wall-mounted pegboard held various tools with specific functions—developer tanks, negative squeegees, bottles of chemicals. It was like a mad scientist's lab, the red light giving a sinister cast. But for as long as he could remember, he enjoyed being in there with Carl while he worked, developing rolls of film.

"Alright, let's see how much damage you did." Carl set the Nikonos on the workbench, pressed the film release, and started cranking the rewind arm. The film made a scratchy, tortured sound inside the camera as it spooled into its canister. "Nice and slow," he said, patiently turning the rewinder. "This film's been in there for a few decades. It could be brittle."

Finally, the sound stopped, and Carl flipped the lock and popped the back release. The camera back hinged open. Carl took an exaggerated sniff. "Smell that? That's the 1970s."

Tusker laughed and took a swig of his beer. He perched on the edge of a tall stool and watched Carl work. Even though he'd made a career as a well-respected nautical engineer, at home Carl was a self-professed luddite who didn't own a smartphone, drove a rusted out but mechanically perfect 1997 Subaru Outback, and had never taken a photo with a digital camera. Tusker gave him a hard time, but at the same time respected him for it.

Carl expertly got the film out of its canister and onto a reel, then inserted it into a developing tank. He mixed the developer solution using a handheld laboratory thermometer and poured it into the small, sealed bucket-shaped tank and swished and swirled it off and on for the next ten minutes, then poured it out and did the same with a fixing solution. Then he flushed the tank with water and finally pulled the top off.

"You can switch on the lights now," he said to Tusker, who did as he was told, flicking a switch to illuminate the room in bright, white light. Carl unspooled the newly processed coil of negatives and clipped it to the drying line. He grabbed a clamp-like rubber squeegee and ran it the length of the strip. Water poured off the end into a drain on the floor. "I know you want to look, but let's go upstairs and have another beer while it dries. Then we can put it on the light table and look at what we've got."

Tusker nodded and they left the darkroom and went upstairs. Carl went straight for the back door, fishing a pack of smokes from the pocket of his flannel shirt. "Filthy habit," he winked, and stepped out onto the back porch. Tusker followed him. Carl extended the pack.

"What the hell," Tusker said and pulled out a Camel Light. Carl lit both of theirs and they puffed quietly, blowing streams of smoky breath into the cold October air. It was 4 p.m. and already getting dark.

"So what do you think is on this film? Any idea?"

"Dunno," Tusker said. "Like I said, it was in that box I found in the shed at the cabin. Guessing it's some underwater stuff, since it's in the Nikonos, and given the vintage of that camera, it's post-Vietnam."

"Huh," Carl said. "You don't suppose it's from that plane

wreck?" He eyed Tusker sideways.

"It could be. When I told Dad's old dive partner about it, he got *real* spooked."

Carl dropped his butt in a coffee can on the porch and turned to go back inside. Tusker followed. They each grabbed a fresh ale and headed back to the darkroom.

Carl clicked on a large lightbox that sat on a drafting table in the corner of the room and tossed a 10x loupe to Tusker, then fetched the negative strip off the drying line. He took a pair of scissors from the pegboard and snipped the strip carefully into two twelve-frame lengths and handed one to Tusker. They stood side by side, hunched over the lightbox, the loupes screwed into their eye sockets.

Most of the photos were badly underexposed and the 800 speed Agfa film had a heavy grain. At first it was impossible to distinguish anything. Only the first frame was clear. It showed a diver in a yellow Mk12 helmet standing on the deck of a ship. Whitecaps were visible in the background and the other men in the photo were dressed in heavy cold weather gear. It must have been Chester Basch, a test photo to make sure the film was advanced to the first frame. Tusker strained to make out the rest of the frames. Then, something familiar in the eighth image: the unmistakable shape of an airplane window. So it was the wreck, he thought.

"Man, if these guys had just had a modern DSLR with 12,000 ISO and some decent strobes back then!" Tusker said in frustration and stood up, rubbing his eyes.

Carl was still hunched over his negatives. He ignored the comment.

"Well, the good news is, I think I can further improve these by enlarging," he said, and finally straightened up and looked at Tusker. "The bad news is, you did manage to expose the last couple of frames when you opened the camera back." Tusker cringed. "But at least you were quick enough to close it again. We've got most of the roll here."

"It is the plane wreck," Tusker said.

"Yup, I saw that too," Carl said. "Looks like your old man was focusing on the tail section. Most of the photos in these last twelve were taken there."

After another beer and smoke break, Carl switched on the red light again and prepared the developer baths and photographic paper. Over the next hour, he worked quietly and intently to make 8x12 enlargements of all the photos. While they were drying, they went upstairs to wait.

The six pack of Two Hearted Ale gone, Carl pulled out a bottle of scotch. It was an old single malt, a twenty-five year-old Dalmore. He produced a pair of Canadian Steamship Line tumblers he'd "liberated" from the shipyard and dosed each of them a two-finger pour.

Tusker whistled. "Wow, feeling generous tonight," he said.

"Seemed appropriate," Carl said. "This whisky is almost as old as that roll of film. Plus, I feel like we're going to need it."

They clinked glasses and Tusker felt the warm scotch slip down his throat. Carl got up and flipped through his cabinet of vinyl records. He pulled one out and dropped the record on the turntable. Tusker heard the familiar crackle, then the opening piano chords of Peter Gabriel's "Here Comes the Flood." Tusker closed his eyes and savored it. The song was the musical equivalent of the whisky he was drinking.

"Figured I'd spare the neighbors this time," Carl smiled.

They reclined there in Carl's cluttered living room, not talking, just listening to the record, sipping their scotch. It was night now, and October nights always seemed darkest, sandwiched as they were between the last twilights of September and the bright snow that comes in November. The only light came from the stereo equalizer and the front porch light filtering through the blinds. When the needle lifted and settled back in its cradle, Carl stood, tipped his glass back to get the last drop and said, "shall we?"

They wandered back to the basement. Carl unclipped the enlarged photos and laid them out on the worktable. He'd manipulated the exposure as much as possible in the developing trays so that the images were a little more clear. Tusker went through each one, setting aside the useless black and blurry ones. The last photo was only half there, with one side almost burned in from sepia to bright white. This was the last usable frame, only partially damaged by his blunder with the Nikonos at the cabin. But there was an object in the corner, clearly the subject of the photo and what his father had aimed to capture.

"What does that look like to you?" Tusker slid the photo over to Carl.

Carl held it up, holding it inches from his face. Then his eyes got big, and he looked at Tusker. His mouth fell open. Tusker grimaced and nodded.

"We need to go dive that plane wreck."

The Loneliest Place on Earth

Marquette, Michigan marina.
Two days later.

"You do know that plane is a gravesite, right?" O'Connell said. "It's illegal to dive it. If the Coasties catch us out there, there'll be a million dollar fine."

"Yup, Carl expressed the same concerns and yours are duly noted also," Tusker said. "And if for some reason we get busted, I'll play the archaeologist card. Research gets a pass—usually."

"Fine, but let's try not to get caught," O'Connell replied. "And if we do, you're paying."

Lake Superior had changed in the week since Tusker was last out on the R/V *Keweenaw* with his students. The calendar had flipped to November and, right on cue, the gales started to blow. There's a reason why it's the deadliest month on the lake, and if the wind and waves could sink monster freighters, the forty-six-foot research and dive boat had no business being out past Marquette's breakwater, much less forty miles offshore.

Tusker had convinced O'Connell to take him and Carl out

to dive the Gulfstream wreck. The Irishman had cut his teeth fishing in the North Atlantic, but he was shaking his head as he gripped the wheel of the *Keweenaw*, his knuckles white. "This is no good," he kept muttering as the boat bashed up and over the six-foot swells that had grown since they left the dock four hours ago. Tusker's attempts at humor fizzled out so he left the captain to concentrate on keeping the bow into the waves.

They'd departed Marquette's marina before sunrise. Tusker left his cabin at 3:30 am, the Scout laden with a double set of steel, one hundred-cubic-foot cylinders of air, two deco bottles of 32% nitrox, and a small stage bottle of pure oxygen. At 190 feet, the wreck would be at the absolute limit of what he was willing to dive on air. Anything deeper would require a helium gas mix to ward off narcosis and oxygen toxicity. He hoped he wouldn't regret his choice.

Between loading the gear, calculating the dive plan, and obsessively consulting a marine forecast app, he'd hardly slept at all. The last-minute discovery of a hole in his dry suit didn't help matters, as he dug out an ancient tube of Aquaseal and dabbed a healthy blob of it on the suit's wound. He hoped it would dry and cure by dive time.

Carl met him at the dock. By the light of their headlamps, they silently loaded the tanks and duffels of gear onto the boat while O'Connell grimly looked on, chain smoking cigarettes. On a good weather day, at eight knots, the *Keweenaw* would make the wreck site's GPS coordinates in four hours. Fighting the huge swells was slow going, and would add close to another hour.

Tusker huddled at the oak galley table inside the boat's cabin, holding onto an ancient Stanley flask of coffee. He was readying the Nauticam underwater camera housing, smearing a thin layer of lubricant on its O-rings, before sliding his Nikon Z7 Mark II inside with a satisfying click. Then he snapped shut the housing's latches and secured the twin Kraken 12,000 lumen lights to their extension arms.

"Not quite a Nikonos, but I guess it'll do," Carl said, gesturing to the oversized rig.

"If only Dad had this setup back in '78," Tusker said. "We wouldn't have had to come all the way out here today," Tusker replied.

On the table was spread a chart of southern Lake Superior. The Stannard Rock Lighthouse was dead center, with fathom soundings radiating out from it. Carl came into the cabin, dripping wet, and slumped onto the bench opposite Tusker. Tusker looked at him and passed the flask across.

"It's not an adventure til something goes wrong," Carl said with a weak grin as he sloshed the coffee into an enamelware camp mug that danced across the pitching table. O'Connell looked away from the spray-streaked windscreen, cigarette dangling from the corner of his lips.

"You guys have your adventures on your own time, thank you very much," he said, his Irish accent more pronounced than usual. "I'm happy if things *don't* go wrong."

Tusker pointed to the lighthouse symbol on the chart. "The wreck is just south of Stannard." He took a blunt carpenter's pencil from a plastic cup and marked an 'X' on the approximate spot.

"Loneliest Place on Earth," Carl said. "Looks like that plane almost clipped the top of the lighthouse, judging by how close it is."

"No kidding," Tusker said. He envisioned the horror of those last moments as the plane careened towards the lake.

"Speak of the devil," O'Connell said, pointing off the bow. Tusker and Carl shimmied out from their benches and peered out the glass, past the overmatched windscreen wipers. As the bow fell from a swell, they could just see a flash through the spray. It was the lighthouse's automated beacon, still ten miles further ahead.

"I can't imagine being a keeper on that rock," Carl said, his eyes fixed on the flashing light.

"Last winter, a window blew out and the Coasties had to send a chopper out to fix it," Tusker said. "They were worried it would expose the electronics inside to the elements."

"Which unlucky rescue swimmer got that job?" Carl said shaking his head.

"They winched him down from the helicopter and he had to chip away half a foot of ice from the door to even get in. The lock was frozen solid, so they had to take a torch to it."

"Alright, chaps, we're closing in on the numbers of this godforsaken wreck," O'Connell throttled back the twin diesels and the boat wallowed. "Who wants to go out front and try to hook the buoy?"

"This is my white whale," Tusker said. "I'll man the harpoon." He had been wearing his polar fleece union suit already and he struggled to keep his footing in the pitching cabin as he climbed into his dry suit. It was a heavy suit from a defunct California company called Diving Concepts. Tusker had worn it for almost twenty years, and it showed in the number of patches and dried clumps of Aquaseal where he'd fixed leaks and tears. He pulled the zipper shut up across his chest and squatted down to force any trapped air out the neck seal.

"If you fall in..." Carl gave him a mischievous look.

"You'll come in after me?"

"Well, I was going to ask if I could have the Scout, but yeah, I'll give it the old college try first."

Tusker thrust up his middle finger and left the cabin. The wind had died down a bit. A good sign. He pulled a long boat hook from a PVC sheath on top of the cabin and shimmied up onto the gunwale, inching his way along the side of the cabin. O'Connell was using the engines to keep the boat stable, but Tusker found it difficult to get his footing on the spray-slicked fiberglass. Finally, he made it onto the bow and knelt down, peering over the rail. He scanned the dark water.

The Gulfstream wreck hadn't been dived since it was declared off limits in 1980, when the investigation closed. That, and its depth and distance from shore, meant that even the most hardcore Great Lakes wreck diver pirates avoided it. But there was a marker buoy, secured to the wreck in '78. Tusker hoped it was still there, not deteriorated by weather or ripped free by a passing freighter. He'd seen it once while doing sonar sweeps, but that was years ago. It was a submerged buoy, meaning the plastic float bobbed about ten feet deep, with a looped mooring line above it.

"There it is!" He shouted back to O'Connell, and pointed in the direction of the buoy, little more than a white plastic bleach bottle. Any fluorescent paint on it had long since faded or washed off. O'Connell maneuvered the *Keweenaw* in the direction Tusker was pointing and managed to coast to a near stop so that it only took one swipe with the boat hook for Tusker to snag the mooring line and tie it into the bow cleat. This was why he was glad O'Connell agreed to drive. He gave a thumbs up. The engine went silent.

"Alright, pal, we've got a window of relatively calm seas here," Tusker said to Carl as he crept back to the aft deck and restowed the boat hook.

Carl was stubbing out a cigarette in his coffee cup. His dry suit was already half on. It was an ancient Parkside Scuba Poseidon Unisuit, bright orange that had faded to more of a tangerine hue. If Tusker's suit was old, Carl's was an antique, a neoprene suit with an integrated hood, chest vent and fill valves, and an ill-conceived crotch zipper that required all manner of contortion to put the suit on. A willing buddy was needed to seal it up, by reaching through your nether regions to pull the zipper shut. It was a constant source of juvenile humor for them whenever they went diving.

"Alright, groper, do your thing," Carl said, standing compliantly with the zipper pull dangling below his crotch. Tusker cackled and got on his knees and yanked. Even O'Connell cracked a smile and framed a shot of the activity with his iPhone's camera.

"If that photo gets made public, I could lose my job at the University!" Tusker said with mock concern.

The humor felt brittle, a mechanism for avoiding the very real danger that awaited them, and once the laughter faded, both divers continued their suiting up rituals quietly. Tusker twisted open both of his tank manifold valves and checked for leaks and puffed in both mouthpieces. He filled his Dive Rite buoyancy wing with enough air to fill out its wrinkles and then slid on his green Force Fin Tan Delta fins. Then came hood and dry gloves, the latter over a thin pair of wool liners. He popped open the Seiko's bracelet extension and slid it over his thick cuff, clipping it shut. Finally, he shimmied his arms through the harness shoulder straps, tightened it all down, and plugged in the dry suit fill valve. He nodded across to Carl who'd been doing a similar operation with his kit. They'd dived together for so many years that they knew each other's rituals and timing and were ready to go into the water.

Tusker sealed his mask on his face and, with great effort, stood on the tossing, slippery deck with close to 200 pounds of gear on his back. He waddled back to the *Keweenaw's* transom. O'Connell helped him down the step and clipped the deco bottles, one on each side of Tusker's harness, and the pure O2 bottle across his chest. Finally, he passed across the Nauticam and Tusker clipped its lanyard to a D-ring on his harness.

Unable to stand there much longer, Tusker gave a half-hearted nod and ungracefully plunged into the foamy lake. He drifted a ways from the boat, waiting for Carl to jump in. When both were in the water, they waved to O'Connell and pulled themselves, hand over hand on the trailing "granny" line to the bow of the boat, then out along the mooring line. Tusker gave one last look around the land of the living. The last thing he saw was a flash on the horizon from Stannard Rock Light. Then he emptied the air from his buoyancy wing and descended into the darkness.

Hard Landing

Lake Superior, 44 nautical miles north of Marquette, Michigan. Present day.

Compared to the surface, the lake's bottom at 194 feet was serene. But it was dark. The sunlight, already filtered behind clouds, barely reached the lakebed, so that it was like a moonless night in a forest.

Tusker fully inflated his buoyancy wing just before touching down on the mud, hovering a few feet above. Time was short. Two tanks wouldn't last long at this depth and every minute they spent would multiply exponentially the amount of decompression time they'd have to spend hanging in the cold water before surfacing. Carl drifted down not far away, giving Tusker a measure of comfort.

Carl wore a rock-climbing helmet over his dry suit hood, and had rigged two high powered Princeton Tec waterproof torches to it, one on each side. This setup, like many wreck diving gear hacks, was derived from the arcane but similar world of cave diving and allowed hands-free exploring as well as some protection in overhead environments. The downside was, whenever he looked at Tusker, he would blind him.

They'd already decided to focus their efforts on the tail end of the Gulfstream. The buoy line was secured near the center of the wreckage, and they had come down close to the left-hand wing. Tusker had dived many shipwrecks, some with the dead bodies of lost crew still entombed inside, but this empty airliner made him shudder. It was a horrifying vision, a plane full of people falling out of the sky, then through fathoms of icy water. As he swam along the rearmost section of ruined fuselage, he swept the twin Kraken lights mounted on his camera rig in an arc. Part of the name, "Overbrook" was still visible, painted above the windows in a decidedly 1970s typeface. The optimism of it was jarring here in the dark.

Finally, the two divers reached the rear of the plane. This is where the fuselage would normally taper down to a cone, with an engine mounted on each side. But where the tail of the plane should be, it looked like a gaping bite wound, like a dorado reeled in on a line, only to find that it was partially taken by a mako.

Tusker decided to make an initial sweep of the fatal maw, then swim in for closer examination. But close examination was all that was possible in the dark. Their powerful torches that, at shallower depths, would turn night into day, cast only a feeble beam here, producing a cone of light that extended maybe six feet. He looked over at Carl but couldn't see his face due to his twin high beams, so he simply shrugged and gestured.

Tusker moved in close to the area where the photos from the Nikonos seemed to focus, the upper left edge of the jagged aluminum of the torn fuselage. In contrast to the thick steel plating of freighter and warship hulls, Tusker was struck by how thin the plane's skin was, built for cabin pressurization and not water resistance. He methodically swept his camera along the entire surface, firing off shots as he went. A 256-gigabyte memory card was a hell of a lot better than a 24-exposure roll of Agfa 800, Tusker thought, as he fired frame after frame. The resulting images on the camera's LCD monitor were crisp and bright. He could see the rivet pattern and reinforcing plates where the tail would have risen out of the fuselage, and here the edge was blackened, clearly burned. Was it merely from an engine explosion, or something else? And where was the object they'd seen in the corner of his father's last photo?

Tusker paused and backed away from the plane a few feet, as far as he could to get perspective while his torches still illuminated the plane. His eyes had adjusted to the dark by now. Looking up, he could see the faintest grey glow from the distant sky above. He mentally traced the edge of the opening from where the lefthand engine would have hung, up to the absent tail. The object, cylindrical in shape and jammed into the thin aluminum, should have been about halfway up. But it wasn't there. Maybe it fell out. After all, the photos were taken over three decades ago.

Tusker turned to Carl, who hovered behind him. As agreed, he was acting as a safety diver so that Tusker could carry out the kind of wreck examination he'd been trained to do as an archaeologist. The twin headlamps lent much-needed light to the scene. Carl pointed at his wrist. Tusker looked at his own dive computer. It was adding up the decompression penalty as he watched it. They were already close to an hour of hang time before they could get back to the relative safety and warmth of the *Keweenaw*. A check of his pressure gauge showed half his air remaining. With his fingers, he indicated how much air he had left, then pointed to his wrist and held his fingers splayed, telling Carl he wanted three minutes longer. The blinding twin torches nodded.

Tusker slowly descended, now into the gaping hole at the rear of the plane. There was a bulkhead, and in front of it, the center aisle of the plane and a few rear seats behind where it had collapsed into a tangle of wiring and debris. The carpeting had long since rotted away but it looked like the scene on any number of commercial air flights he'd been on, flying to Washington, Sri Lanka, or Jamaica. He scanned the floor below him, hoping to catch sight of the object. He took a few photos, hoping that later analysis might turn up something he was missing. It was a jumbled, chaotic mess of debris. For a moment, he considered that his father had been in this exact place, with a camera, forty years earlier. It was the only wreck he was certain they both had dived. And it was the one that ended up slowly killing him. He shuddered and started to refocus on his task, pulling at the heaps of debris, hoping to find a clue. That was a mistake.

A huge plume of silt, accumulated over decades on the lake bottom, rose in slow motion from the debris and immediately created a whiteout. Tusker's torch beams became a liability, much as high beam headlamps are when driving in fog. He hadn't intended to penetrate the wreck so didn't bring a reel or safety line, and now he found himself disoriented inside the crashed plane. He kicked and one of his fins became momentarily wedged under a seat. He bent to dislodge it and knocked open what he recognized as a seatback tray table. He tried to regulate his breathing. He'd been here before, countless times, inside a wreck, entangled, disoriented. *Remember your training!*

A hand on his shoulder, then tugging on his tank manifold. Tusker spun around in the cloud and lashed out, his gloved hand meeting rubber and neoprene. He heard a grunt, then the grip on his shoulder was more firm. Tusker struggled to get away. He reached for his knife. Then a blow to his arm before he could pull it from its sheath on his lower leg. He was back there, back in Sri Lanka, in the bowels of the *Vampire*, fighting an invisible foe. A hose, a valve, anything to compromise this diver, then swim out, get to the surface! His heart pounded and he could hear it inside his own thick hood. He gasped for air. Then he went blind.

Tusker's eyes went white behind closed lids. When he opened them, the brightness didn't go away. His retinas were seared, and his head pounded. *This is it,* he thought, *I'm finished.* He felt himself go limp and surrendered to his fate. As he slowly drifted down inside the wreck, his fin brushed something long and cylindrical, with four twisted pieces of metal on one end. The object tumbled down, unseen, and settled below a collapsed row of seats, lost once again.

Land Of The Living

Onboard the R/V Keweenaw, Lake Superior.
The same day.

"Dude, you need a new therapist!" Those were the first words out of Carl's mouth as they surfaced. In the ninety minutes they'd been underwater, Lake Superior had turned into an ugly, turbulent maelstrom. The sky's muscular, dark surface was reflected back by the swells, which were topped with lashes of whitecaps.

"Anger issues, my man, anger issues," Carl went on. Tusker didn't reply. He was entirely spent, visibly shaking as he struggled to stay upright in his heavy rig. Carl saw that he was in trouble and swam to him. He pressed the fill valves on Tusker's buoyancy wing and dry suit, unclipped one of his empty deco bottles, and then started swimming with it towards the *Keweenaw*. "Come on, man, swim!" His tone had turned deadly serious.

O'Connell, as soon as the divers surfaced, had scampered onto the bow and untied from the mooring, releasing the boat from its tortured tether. He fired the diesels and made wide arcs around the divers in an attempt to flatten the surface waves. Then he expertly backed the transom to where they bobbed. He had no idea what had transpired since they last saw him, but he could tell something was wrong.

Carl deftly climbed the Christmas tree swim ladder in his fins and dumped his gear in one motion, dropping deco bottles, unclipping shoulder straps and twisting out of his heavy harness before handing the heavy Nauticam camera rig he'd taken from Tusker to O'Connell. Then he immediately jumped back in the water to help Tusker. He grabbed his tank manifold and pulled him, swimming a labored side stroke to the ladder, where he reached under and unclipped Tusker's harness and pulled it out from under him. O'Connell was there to grab it and heave it on to the transom before bounding back to the wheel to keep the boat steady. Tusker, unburdened, feebly climbed the ladder and collapsed onto the dive deck bench. Carl knelt and pulled his fins off for him, then undid the cross-body zipper. Tusker gave him a weak smile and a nod.

"We all secure back there?" O'Connell shouted. Carl gave him an OK sign and the captain pushed the throttles forward. The *Keweenaw* labored as the revs climbed. With a trailing wind and following seas, at least the trip back should go faster, O'Connell thought, as he lit his twentieth cigarette of the day.

Carl and Tusker sat on the dive deck benches, out in the wind, both with dry suits half open, staring at each other silently. Finally, Carl spoke.

"Narc'd?"

Nitrogen narcosis is a phenomenon unknown to those

who never breathe compressed air deep underwater. Cousteau called it "the rapture of the deep," but it is anything but rapturous. At lesser depths, a diver can feel like he's drunk a couple of stiff cocktails. But at greater depths, it can result in confusion, paranoia, or full-on terror. The narcotic effect is a result of the nitrogen in the breathing gas, over 70% of normal air, which is concentrated under the extreme pressure at which it is delivered to the diver's lungs. Deep divers often opt for more exotic gas mixes to mitigate this effect, replacing much or all of the nitrogen with helium. But Tusker and Carl had decided to dive on air. And what had happened had nothing to do with nitrogen.

"I… I don't know. I don't think so," Tusker said, softly. He knew it wasn't that. "I've been…" He considered telling Carl the truth, that he'd had these attacks ever since coming home from Sri Lanka. But instead, he said, "I haven't been sleeping well lately. And you know, no such thing as an old, bold diver, and all that. Maybe I'm just past my prime."

"Too much tropical diving is what I think it is," Carl grinned. But he knew. And Tusker knew that he knew. Panic underwater is a primal thing. There's no disguising it, and all who see it never forget it. Carl would never see him the same way again. Now he was weak, compromised, unreliable. He'd tried to stab Carl, for Christ's sake!

How Carl managed to drag him out of that airplane, Tusker would never know. He'd been in a full-blown panic, his primal instincts driving his actions, his addled brain thinking he was in the bowels of a World War II warship off the coast of Sri Lanka. The reality was, Carl's headlamps had blinded Tusker, somehow paralyzing him long enough for Carl to drag him back out of the silted-up ass end of the Gulfstream and start an awkward ascent.

Carl had to stick close and not only vent his own buoyancy wing, but also Tusker's to prevent a runaway ascent from the rapidly expanding air. He had reached across and unclipped the dangling camera rig from Tusker's D-ring and transferred it to his own harness. By the time they reached their first decompression stop at ninety feet, Tusker had regained some of his senses—enough to stay calm and take direction. They floated there, neutrally buoyant, making eye contact. Tusker looked vacant, drugged, and Carl held him by both shoulders, like a father and son having a heart to heart, or a priest giving a benediction.

By sixty feet, Tusker was coherent enough to switch over to his nitrox decompression bottle. Its 32% oxygen, which would have been toxic if breathed on the bottom, had provided a clearer head and faster decompression than the air in his primary tanks.

By fifteen feet, they were breathing off their small pure O2 bottles. Both men shivered, as much from an adrenaline hangover as the thirty-seven degree water. They hung there, with the shadow of the *Keweenaw* just above them, for twenty minutes, until their oxygen bottles were near zero. Decompression dives have as much of a ceiling as a cave or shipwreck—it's simply invisible. Time itself prevents a diver from surfacing, no matter how badly he wants, or needs, to get back to air and sunlight. To break that ceiling risks an almost certain case of the bends.

The boat ride back to Marquette was torturous for all three men. O'Connell looked haggard from riding out the swells and the stress of trying to keep his boat upright and afloat. Tusker sat huddled in every layer of clothing he'd brought. Despite his patching, his dry suit had leaked, cold lake water pooling in both of the attached boots and halfway up his legs. Carl sat in the doorway, looking back at the fading flash of Stannard Rock, smoking. When it was out of sight, he got up and pulled a flask out of his battered dive bag. He simply passed it over to Tusker, who nodded and unscrewed the lid. It was the old Dalmore again and he took a healthy pull.

Carl took it from him and extended it to O'Connell who looked briefly and shook his head. "Just a nip, captain," Carl smiled. "We won't tell anyone. It'll calm your nerves." O'Connell took the flask and tipped it back, taking more than a nip.

"It's not Irish, but it'll do," he said and passed the flask back.

It was dark by the time they saw the red and green lights of the Marquette marina breakwater. With the exception of a couple of downbound lake freighters in the distance and a lone Coast Guard cutter, they'd not seen another vessel all day. The Coast Guard boat had raised them on the radio and asked what they were up to, out in such a gale. O'Connell lied and simply said, "just shuffling boats for the end of season," secretly hoping he'd not have to put out a distress call from forty miles out.

Inside the marina, the water was mercifully calm, and the *Keweenaw* finally tied up at her slip at 6:30 p.m. Tusker and Carl heaved their wet gear in a jumble by the dock, then drove the Scout and Subaru down to load up. O'Connell tidied up his boat, plugged it in to shore power, and stood watching the two divers work.

"I'd offer to buy you a beer, but I suspect you'd like to get on home," Tusker said to the Irishman. O'Connell nodded, gave a small salute to them both, and ambled off towards the parking lot.

With their vehicles loaded, Carl lit a cigarette and leaned on the hood of the Scout. The two men looked out at the twinkling lights of town across the water. The sound of semi-trucks engine braking down Washington Street mingled with the tinkling of lines on the few boats remaining in the marina, and the crash of the waves on the breakwater.

"I guess I never asked if you found what you hoped to down there," Carl said finally.

Tusker just shook his head. "I need to make another visit to Chester," he said. "He knows something he's not telling me."

"You know, we all have rough patches," Carl said softly. "God knows, I have. And if you ever need to talk..."

"Thanks, man," Tusker said, cutting him off.

"Now, diving is another story," Carl said with a grin. "You're gonna need to find another victim for that." He patted Tusker hard on his shoulder and stepped towards the Subaru. "Take care of yourself now."

"I will," Tusker said. "Trust me, I will. And thanks for saving my life out there."

Carl nodded up to him from the driver's seat and started the car. He switched on the headlamps, and made a wide U-turn, driving up the steep driveway out of the marina. Tusker climbed into the Scout, which now smelled of wet dive gear mixed with gearbox oil. He turned the key, put the truck in first, and aimed for the cabin. He had a two-hour drive ahead of him, and could think of nothing but sleep.

Our Lady of Discomfort

Marquette. Michigan.
That same night.

The night nurse at the care home had been surprised to see the tall woman approach the reception desk. She hadn't heard her come in, and there were typically few visitors after 8 p.m.

"Family member?" she dutifully asked, noticing the woman was Black, and remembering that Chester Basch was their only African-American resident.

The woman nodded but didn't say anything, already bent over signing the visitor's log in an illegible script. The nurse pointed to the last room on the corridor. The woman didn't thank her, but strode quietly down the hall. She was tall and broad-shouldered and wore masculine clothes—tall boots, tactical cargo pants and a zip-up track jacket with the hood pulled up, all black. The nurse went back to studying her iPhone.

The room was dark, its only light emanating from a small television in the corner—a college basketball game, volume turned low. Chester Basch sat in his recliner facing the TV. He was half asleep. He liked to sit up and watch the late news, one of the few rituals he'd kept since coming to Our Lady of Comfort.

He didn't hear the woman enter his room. Suddenly, she was standing over him. He looked up, startled by her appearance. Her eyes were somehow different—one caught a reflection from the TV, shimmering silver or blue. The other was black, showing no iris at all. Somehow Chester had been expecting a visit. His hand slowly slid towards the nurse call button on its tether at his side. The woman bent close, reaching across equally slowly and closing her own hand around his. She squeezed, hard. Chester grimaced and opened his mouth. With her other hand, the woman covered it. Chester's eyes widened. She let go of his hand and tossed the call button on the floor, then reached over and increased the TV volume using its remote.

"What did you tell Tusk?" she hissed in his ear, slowly releasing her grip on his mouth. He shook his head but didn't say anything. She reached behind him and he heard a hiss. She had shut off his oxygen supply. His breathing became labored.

"One more try," she said again, calmly. "What did you tell Tusk?"

"Tell Hockenheimer to go to hell!" Chester hissed and swung his arm. The Tudor watch on his wrist connected with the woman's nose. She grunted and released him. Blood poured down her face. Chester tried to get up but he was too weak, and his oxygen hose had snagged across the back of the big chair. She pounced on him, seething now. Her face was a mess of blood and the one living eye burned with fury, the other still cold and gray. She ripped the rubber oxygen tube from around his ears and from his nose and, in one motion, coiled its length twice around his neck. Chester looked into her face, knowing it was the last one he would ever see.

The woman held him against the chair with one massive forearm and twisted the rubber tubing with her other hand. A croaking sound came from Chester's mouth. Years ago, in Navy dive training in Chicago, he'd practiced out of air emergencies, breath-hold diving, and emergency ascents from as deep as a hundred feet. He'd once been able to hold his breath for over four minutes. But not anymore. Chester Basch, Diver, Second Class, and former Underwater Demolition Team member, was dead.

The reception nurse was surprised again when the woman reappeared such a short time later. She walked swiftly past the desk, holding a tissue over her face, head down.

"You need to sign out, please!"

The woman ignored her and was gone, out into the cold night.

Home Invasion

Lac La Belle.
Later the same night.

Tusker hadn't left the lights on in the cabin. He never did. He could see it through the trees even before he turned down the driveway, a solitary light twinkling from the kitchen window. He switched off the Scout's headlamps and drove past, parking in a roadside ditch about a quarter mile beyond. He clawed through his dive bag in the dark truck and found his Wenoka knife, the one he'd almost used to stab Carl, the one with which he'd killed two men back in Sri Lanka last year. It was supposed to be used to cut old fishing line, not disembowel people or cut air hoses. But it was quickly becoming his weapon of choice.

He climbed down from the driver's seat and slowly shut the door without latching it. Then he sprinted up the soft shoulder of the gravel road, hugging the line of balsam firs and white pines so their shadows hid his. The wind was still up, and the rustle of branches and dead leaves disguised his foot fall as he approached the top of the driveway. There wasn't a vehicle there, nor any new tire tracks that he could see. Maybe he was being paranoid. Maybe he had left the light on when he left in the wee hours that morning to make the long drive to Marquette.

He skirted around the back of the cabin, to the lake side. He crouched down as he passed the window below the cabin's single big room. He saw a shadow pass across the shaft of light that lit up the ground. Tusker waited, counting to three before slowly raising his head above the window ledge to look inside. At first, he didn't see anyone, but the cabin was a scene of chaos. Every shelf had been emptied, every book was on the floor. Papers were scattered on the table, the kitchen drawers open and empty of their contents.

Then, he saw a figure. It was a tall person dressed all in black—tactical pants, lace up boots, a jacket with a hood that obscured the face, even gloves. The intruder's back was to the window, and they were peering at the bright screen of a smart phone. Tusker stood up further, straining to get a better look. It was no use. He gripped the knife in his left hand and continued around to the porch. It was dark back there and he could hear the waves on Lac La Belle. The lake was no Superior, but when the wind came across, it could kick up some whitecaps. But he didn't look at the lake. He focused on the porch's screen door on its flimsy wooden frame. The screen had so many holes in it by now, it offered no protection from summer's mosquitoes. Patching it would be another off-season job.

When Tusker reached the door, he found its screen had been neatly cut in a right angle, flapping open in the wind. He never locked the back door of the cabin. Latched with a single hook, the screen door was more of a deterrent for the odd bear, latched to keep the wind from opening it. But this was how the intruder had entered. He stepped on the first of the three wooden steps. They were creaky, he knew, and he was careful not to make a sound. Then the second step. Still quiet. Then the top step and through the door. But something wasn't right. His shin caught on something, a thin wire of some sort, and before he registered what it was, there was a loud clatter. He stumbled, caught his balance with his right arm, and started to get up.

Just then, the back door flew open and caught Tusker square on the shoulder. He reeled backwards as the intruder rushed past him and out the door. Off balance, Tusker lunged with his knife hand. The razor sharp edge of the blade got purchase, and he pushed and swiped. He heard a shout of pain, but the intruder disappeared into the darkness towards the lake, moving fast. Tusker got to his feet and pushed through the now obliterated porch door and gave chase, but the intruder had a head start. He heard an outboard motor fire. That's why he hadn't seen a car in the driveway. As Tusker got to the dock, slippery with spray, he saw a black rigid inflatable skiff angling away, the dark figure silhouetted against the night sky, standing in the back, one hand on the motor's throttle, the other clutching a bicep, and looking back at Tusker.

Tusker looked at the little Alumacraft fishing boat tied up to the other side of the dock and briefly considered giving chase. But in this weather, with the boat's antique Evinrude outboard, it wouldn't even be close. He listened as the sound of the motor grew distant, its pitch rising and falling as it bounced over the swells, now invisible in the stormy darkness.

He made his way back up to the cabin. Inside the porch, he pulled the cord to switch on the hanging light and saw what had given him away: a simple trip wire alarm strung across the threshold, one end tied around the leg of a stool. Clever, he thought. This person knew what he was doing. Or was it *she*? He remembered Hockenheimer's bodyguard, the menacing woman. The tall frame with broad shoulders seemed to fit, but it was dark and he hadn't seen a face. The yelp when he sliced through flesh with the Wenoka did sound more… feminine? He filed it away in case he ever saw her again.

The inside of the cabin was a mess. He didn't even know where to begin. *I should call the police,* Tusker thought. But it was late, he was tired and hungry, and his nerves still worn raw from the dive on the Gulfstream, the rough boat ride, and the long drive home. It could wait until morning. He made a cursory survey of the damage. The intruder didn't seem to be carrying anything out when they ran, and despite the chaos, Tusker didn't notice anything that was missing. The fact is, the cabin didn't hold much of value to a burglar. Although no photos were still on the wall, they'd been left strewn on the floor, some out of their frames. His Zeiss spotting scope remained on its tripod by the big picture window that looked out on the lake. Even the Chelsea ship's clock remained, dutifully ticking on the wall over the small desk, whose drawers were all emptied of their old letters, bills, and photographs. *Photographs.*

Tusker started sifting through the pile on the desk. There was the envelope of pictures he'd taken to show Chester last week. He thumbed through them. A handful were missing—the ones he'd developed with Carl. The ones from the Nikonos. *So that's what they were after*, he thought. It was all dawning on him slowly, as if pieces of a puzzle were being revealed one at a time, or a shipwreck uncovered, little by little.

He looked up at the old Morse Mk 12 diving helmet, still sitting in its place of pride on the built-in bookcase behind the sofa, one of the few things left undisturbed in the cabin, probably because it was so heavy. It had been his father's when he worked with the Navy's MDSU, worn the very last time he'd been underwater. Tusker walked over to it. The fiberglass was scratched and badly gouged, evidence of its history of use.

Tusker reached out and slowly lifted the front edge of the helmet, where it sat on the wood. He reached underneath, feeling around inside with his hand until he found what he was looking for. He smiled, wrapped his fingers around it, and pulled it out of the helmet: a small envelope of Agfa 800 film negatives.

Dark Roast

Marquette. Michigan.
The next day.

Tusker was already on his second cup of Taconite dark roast when he heard the deep rumble of the Royal Enfield. Leila Mansour was anything but subtle. Everyone in the Oreboat Café paused their conversations until the motorcycle's engine was finally shut off.

Tusker had taken a table in the front corner by the big window that faced the street, and he could see Leila maneuver the bike to an angled parking spot at the curb, just in front of his Scout and behind a small Kia sedan. She took off her helmet, revealing a black wool balaclava that covered all but her eyes. She pulled that off and shook out her hair. It was, by now, genuinely cold—early November cold—and there were no other motorcycles on the roads of the Upper Peninsula. Tusker smiled to himself and shook his head out of respect.

Leila swung open the door of the cafe, clanging its bell loudly. Again, conversation paused and heads swiveled. She surveyed the cafe, spotted Tusker, and strode across to his table.

"Been here long?" she smiled mischievously, knowing she was twenty minutes late.

"Fairly," he smiled back, glancing at his watch.

"Sorry, it's been a morning," she said without further explanation. "Looks like you're set for caffeine. Just let me grab something and I'll be right back." She set her helmet and dispatch bag down on the table, flung her leather jacket over an empty chair and walked back to the service counter.

Been a morning, Tusker thought. *Wait til I tell her about my day.* He studied her as she stood waiting for her drink, bantering with the barista. She was slightly built, but stood tall with legs apart and shoulders back, with a confidence that occupied a bigger space. Her padded leather motorcycle pants and tall boots accentuated her shape and he caught himself staring. He hadn't really thought about being with a woman for, how long was it, over a year since Samanthi had left?

Leila returned with a steaming mug of something. Tusker smelled some kind of spice. She set it down and sat on the chair opposite Tusker.

"Let me guess—chai?" He gestured to her cup.

"Yeah, but they didn't have oat milk, just soy," she replied, slightly annoyed. "Anything is better than dairy, so it'll do."

Tusker looked sheepishly down at his coffee with its splash of cream. The dairy industry was probably another target of her ire. Then again, maybe she was just lactose intolerant.

Leila leaned forward exaggeratedly, elbows on the table, chin in hands. "Anyway, I'm all yours," she said, eyes widening, then pulled back and laughed. "No really, tell me about your exciting evening. You were pretty vague on the phone."

As Tusker recounted the past 24 hours — the dive on the Gulfstream, minus his panic attack, and the intruder at his house — Leila listened with rapt and ever more serious attention.

"Clearly you're getting too close to something that someone wants to stay hidden," she said. "And I'd be willing to bet that someone is Senator Theodore Hockenheimer."

"I've been coming to the same conclusion," Tusker said. He lifted his mug to his lips, then noticed it was empty again and set it down. "The person in my cabin last night had the same build as his bodyguard, that big woman from the park the other day."

"Hockenheimer likes to surround himself with these scary goons, former Special Forces types. He's well connected from his time in the Navy and on the Armed Services Committee."

"For what it's worth, I did manage to cut the person's arm, so if it was that bodyguard, she'd have a pretty nasty wound to show for it."

"Not sure how you'd get close enough to her to find out," Leila said. "Unless you plan to seduce her. You do know how to do that, don't you?" She grinned, and her eyes twinkled flirtatiously.

"I'm not sure she's the seduce-able type," Tusker said. A silence hung between them across the table, both of them smiling and looking at each other, the din of the cafe's other conversations filling the space with white noise. Finally, Tusker broke the tension.

"I found some photos," he said, his tone turning serious. "Near as I can tell, they're from my father's last dive, when he was investigating the crash of Overbrook's plane."

"What do they show? Can I see them?" Leila said excitedly, squirming in her chair.

"Most are pretty unrecognizable, but one of them seems to show some kind of…" Tusker suddenly felt ridiculous mentioning it, "missile."

Leila's jaw dropped and her eyes widened. She sat back and looked out the window. "This is big, really big," she said and took a pen and ratty Moleskine notebook out of her dispatch bag. She thumbed the pages, settling on one, scanning it. Her voice lowered to nearly a whisper.

"There was an eyewitness account back in '78 from a fisherman on the lake who swears he saw," she read from the notebook, "'a streak in the sky followed by a fireball.' No one took him seriously, and then, after the official report, the whole story just disappeared."

"I took a camera down with me on the dive yesterday. The photos are much better than my dad's, but the wreck has deteriorated a lot since he was there, and I can't find anything conclusive. But the pattern of damage and the burn marks seem suspicious to me."

Leila was writing furiously on a fresh page in her notebook. Tusker waited until she stopped and looked up, before continuing.

"But my question is, if Chester Basch and my dad saw something suspicious enough to take photos of the wreck, and there was an eyewitness, why didn't that make it into the crash report?" Tusker said. "As far as I know, they never even went back to the wreck after those dives in late '78. Ice cover on Superior later that winter reached 94 percent and all shipping was stopped. After the report came out, the whole story just died out. They said diving it was too dangerous, held some sort of wreath laying over the wreck site, and that was that. Then it was declared a gravesite, and no one was allowed to dive it."

"Seems like Chester and your dad had the key to the whole investigation." Leila drained her cup. "But the fact that they never told anyone about it, or showed those photos..."

"He did get pretty messed up on that last dive," Tusker interrupted. "I was just a little kid, but I remember he was in the hospital for months, and then a wheelchair after that."

"But he'd still have been able to say something," Leila

replied. "And what about Chester? He would have seen whatever was down there. And why not get that film developed?"

"I tried to ask Chester about it, but he got really weird," Tusker said. "Told me to forget the whole thing. That's why I decided to go dive the Gulfstream."

"Maybe your photos will prompt a new investigation," Leila said. "We can run them with a story…"

"One problem," Tusker cut her off. "Technically my photos are illegal. The wreck site has been restricted for diving since 1980."

Leila frowned. "How convenient," she said. "I suspect the honorable senator from the state of Michigan had a hand in that. I also bet he had something on your dad and Chester to keep them from talking. They were all in the Navy after all. With your dad… er, gone, that just leaves Chester."

"And now me," Tusker said. Leila didn't say anything but she knew it too.

"Sounds like we need to pay Chester another visit," she said.

Sweetwater

Great Lakes National Cemetery, Holly, Michigan.
One week later.

The funeral was sparsely attended. This was partly due to the fact that not many of Chester Basch's old Navy buddies were still alive, and because most of his family relations lived in North Carolina. Only a handful made the trip to Holly, Michigan for the ceremony. Chester had divorced his wife, Lydia, shortly after returning from Vietnam, and never remarried. He liked to say he never had kids, adding with a chuckle, "that I know of."

Still, Lydia was there, standing at the grave site in a long black wool coat. She'd reconnected with Chester in recent years, occasionally visiting him at the nursing home when she was in the U.P. They'd made the sort of peace that the elderly often do, knowing that it's no good taking grudges to the grave. The Navy sent a chaplain and honor guard, with a full military funeral, complete with a three-volley salute and a folded flag for Lydia.

Tusker and Leila made the long drive down to Holly to pay their respects. Against his better judgment, Tusker had picked up Leila in the Scout at the Landmark Inn, where she was staying in Marquette. He considered leaving the old truck behind and taking his Toyota pickup, but the Scout had been running well, and a small, juvenile part of him wanted to impress Leila with it. It was the first time Tusker had seen her dressed in anything but her motorcycle gear.

"You clean up nicely," he'd said when she came out of the hotel and climbed into the truck. She was wearing a long black sweater with a thick turtleneck collar, a charcoal skirt and tall, black, zip-up leather boots.

"We do our best," she smiled.

A week earlier, they'd gone to see Chester Basch at Our Lady of Comfort only to be told that he'd died the night before, the same night Tusker's cabin had been ransacked. The two events were impossible to separate, despite the fact that the nursing home hadn't found anything strange about his death.

"He died in his sleep," the nurse at the reception desk had told them. Tusker and Leila took a look around his room, but it had already been cleaned out, ready for the next guest. A small pile of cardboard boxes stood in the corner, taped shut and addressed to Lydia.

Great Lakes National Cemetery had an appropriate setting, its rows of stark gravestones solemnly lined up on rolling green hills overlooking a small lake. Chester Basch was to be the 23,411th member of the Armed Forces interred there. It was a raw day with low, scudding clouds, somehow befitting a November funeral for a Navy man. Tusker and Leila stood respectfully across the grave from Lydia, a man introduced as Chester's cousin, a young couple with a squirming toddler, and a handful of old men in uniforms and overcoats. Tusker had considered dusting off his father's wool Navy dress coat but thought better of it. He'd never served, so it seemed disrespectful. He'd opted instead for a dark suit, thankful it still fit since the last time he'd worn it. In lieu of an overcoat, he'd worn woolen long johns underneath, and tucked a watch cap into his pocket in case the wind picked up.

The chaplain gave a forgettable speech and benediction. Clearly, he had never met Chester, and the words sounded generic. Tusker's mind wandered as he shifted his weight from foot to foot in his uncomfortable black brogues. "Died in his sleep," he thought. Chester hadn't seemed particularly strong when he'd visited him the week prior, but he was hardly on death's door. The nursing home would have had no reason to suspect anything and likely had a waiting list for rooms, so any investigation would be an unwanted inconvenience.

Tusker's eyes were downcast, looking at the coffin while he considered what to do next, when he felt Leila's hand creep into his, intertwine fingers, and give a squeeze. Not what he'd expected, especially here. He looked over at her and gave a small, reassuring smile, but she was not looking at him. Instead, she was staring straight ahead, her eyes laser focused past the gathered mourners. Tusker followed her gaze and realized why she'd gotten his attention. Across the grass, a black Chevy Suburban had parked on the roadside. Ted Hockenheimer had arrived.

The presidential candidate stood outside the SUV, the imposing bodyguard at his side, wearing the same black tactical outfit that she had at the park in Marquette, the same sunglasses covering her eyes. What was the senator doing here? Was it a publicity stunt? Hardly a good place for it, given Chester's relative anonymity and the tiny crowd of gathered mourners. There was no press, besides Leila, to notice him there, no photo ops.

When the chaplain finished his ramblings, the honor guard fired off their salute, the cracks of their rifles piercing the brittle autumn air. A lieutenant approached Lydia Basch and presented her with a folded American flag, and she nodded her thanks. The crowd started to disperse, some clapping each other on the back, some approaching Lydia to offer condolences, then filing across the fading grass to their vehicles. Tusker and Leila were about to approach her when Hockenheimer strode across purposefully and took her by the elbow. Tusker saw him bend over and whisper something to her. He placed one hand on her stooped shoulder. Then he slipped his other hand inside his own woolen overcoat and pulled out what looked like a white envelope. He handed it to Lydia, who seemed flustered. She hesitantly took it from him and slid it into her purse.

Tusker stepped forward just as the senator straightened up and turned to leave.

"Senator, how kind of you to make an appearance at a veteran's funeral," he said. Hockenheimer looked from Tusker to Leila and back at Tusker.

"Chester Basch was a war hero, and a groundbreaking Black American. He deserves full honors and everyone's respect."

"So you knew him personally?" Leila broke in. The senator fixed her with a glare that softened into a half smile.

"We crossed paths in service. As did your father and I, Mr. Tusk." He turned to Tusker. "They don't make men like Chester Basch and Jonathan Tusk anymore."

"Did you serve with them in Vietnam?" Tusker asked. "I don't recall my father ever mentioning your name."

"Not directly," Hockenheimer said. "But the Underwater Demolition Teams were part of my command."

"And later, the Mobile Diving and Salvage Unit?" Tusker shot back. The senator's cheeks went red.

"No, I was out of the Navy by the time your father and Captain Basch had moved into the MDSU."

"Ah, yes, running for Senate then, if I recall," Leila chimed in. Hockenheimer gave an enigmatic smile.

The bodyguard leaned in behind the senator and whispered something in his ear.

"Yes, Slider, I'll only be a minute."

Tusker looked at Slider. Was she the intruder at his cabin?

There was no way of telling if she had a knife wound on her arm under the thick jacket. She was the right build and height for the person he'd seen running to the dock that night. Though he couldn't see her eyes behind the sunglasses, he could tell she was sizing him up.

"Nice of you to come for the funeral as well," Hockenheimer said to Tusker. "I didn't realize you were close to Chester Basch."

"Oh, I've known Chester a long time," Tusker replied. "In fact, I only just saw him last week and he seemed OK. His death seemed rather sudden." His eyes moved to Slider, who didn't react.

"Yes, so unfortunate," Hockenheimer said, turning to leave. "His emphysema must have been much worse than anyone suspected."

"Something like that," Tusker said, bitterly.

"If you'll excuse me, Mr. Tusk and Ms. Mansour, I have a flight to catch back to Washington. Take good care, both of you." He smiled again, his teeth far too white. Then he turned to walk towards the SUV.

Suddenly, Tusker had an idea. It was a risk, but he did it anyway. With three quick, silent strides, he came up behind Hockenheimer, reaching out to grasp his arm. The senator spun around and, in the same instant, so did Slider. She stepped between Tusker and her charge, putting her left arm out to block Tusker's access. It was a classic close protection officer's move, but Tusker had anticipated it and reached up and gripped her bicep through the sleeve of her jacket. She winced and yelped in pain. Tusker let go and backed away. Slider regained her composure and squared up to Tusker, reaching with her right hand into her jacket for something.

"Slider! Enough." Hockenheimer said, firmly. The bodyguard slowly returned her hand to her side and simply stared at Tusker as she walked slowly backwards, following the senator to his waiting SUV. Tusker gave a smirk and a small wave. He had his answer.

"Julian, is everything OK?" Tusker spun around, remembering where he was. It was Lydia. She was standing next to Leila, a few yards behind him. She'd seen the whole exchange but seemed confused.

"I'm fine, Lydia," he said, giving a reassuring smile. "Just fine."

"It really is nice to see you after all these years," she said softly, with a sad smile. "And a shame it had to be Chester's death that brings us together." Lydia looked much older than the last time Tusker had seen her. *When was that?* Probably his own father's funeral. Despite a pronounced stoop and a full head of white hair, she'd retained the slim elegance he'd remembered. She wore a floral silk scarf around her neck, adding a flash of color to her funeral black.

"Yes, a real shame," Tusker replied, not really knowing what to say. He hadn't known her well at all, only vaguely recalling that she was living in Auburn Hills, near Detroit, and had been a dance teacher at one of the city's art colleges.

"Well, thank you for coming," she said warmly and started slowly walking towards the cemetery road and her car. She stopped and turned. "Chester was so fond of your father, and of you. He talked about you, you know. Said if he'd had a son, he'd wished he'd be like 'Jonny's boy'."

"That's incredibly kind. I had no idea," Tusker said.

"I got some boxes of his belongings from the nursing home. They're in the trunk of my car." She gestured to an ancient diesel Mercedes parked nearby. The car was immaculate. "There's a box in there with your name on it and a note asking me to pass it on to you."

Tusker raised his eyebrows and looked at Leila, who shrugged. They walked over to the car, and Lydia opened the trunk. There were the same boxes Tusker and Leila had seen at Our Lady of Comfort last week. Inside an open one was a smaller box with the name "Julian" scrawled in unsteady Sharpie. She pointed to it and Tusker lifted it out, delicately as if it were a precious or fragile object.

"Whatever it is, it must be special or important, because he had called me the day before he died and left a message," Lydia said. "He said that it had to get to Jonathan Tusk's boy. It's odd, as if he knew he was going to die."

"I suspect he did," Tusker said sadly and gave Lydia a stiff hug. She held on a little bit longer, then backed away.

"Will you come back to the house for a bit of lunch? I've made some bites for Chester's cousins who came up from Carolina."

Tusker took her hand. "No, thank you, Lydia. We have a long drive back up to Marquette so better get on the road." He nodded towards the old Scout, as if it were an excuse. Lydia nodded in understanding, and they waved as she started the Mercedes and slowly rattled away.

Tusker and Leila climbed into the Scout and sat quietly there for a while. He started the truck, letting the engine idle enough to generate some warmth from its heater.

"I have no doubt Hockenheimer's bodyguard was the intruder at my cabin last week," Tusker finally said.

"And I also suspect she was the cause of old Chester's demise," Leila said, looking over at him. Tusker nodded and put the Scout in gear. The truck slowly made its way through the tree lined road and towards the cemetery's exit. "Well, don't you want to open it?" Leila asked, gesturing to the box on the seat between them.

"Go ahead," Tusker said, reaching across and fishing a Swiss Army knife out of the truck's glovebox. Leila opened the blade and cut the tape that sealed the flaps of the box. She propped it up on her lap and opened it. Tusker looked over his shoulder and stepped on the accelerator. The Scout's V8 responded with a rumble as they merged onto I-75 North.

The box was nearly empty, and Leila pulled out the contents—some newspaper clippings, a photocopy of some sort of report, and a small cloth pouch with something weighty inside. She set the papers aside on the seat and opened the drawstring of the pouch. She lifted its contents out like she would a worm or a dead fish.

"It's… a watch," she said, displaying it to Tusker, who took his eyes off the traffic briefly to study it. It was Chester's old Tudor, instantly recognizable by the wide steel cuff band he'd had custom made for him in the Philippines while on leave from Vietnam.

Tusker whistled softly and raised his eyebrows. "Wow, that's a real treasure," he said. "A watch and a knife were really the only two prized possessions a UDT diver had back in the day." He felt a spasm of sadness, remembering how his father had given him the Aquastar he'd worn as a Navy Diver, the watch Tusker had lost at the bottom of the Indian Ocean.

"Looks pretty beat up," Leila said. She turned it over in her hands, studying it.

"Battle scars," Tusker said. "If that watch could talk."

"Well, maybe it can," she said. "There's something engraved on the inside of the band."

It was getting dark outside. Tusker flicked on the Scout's dim headlamps. It would be a long, dark drive back to Marquette.

"What does it say?"

"I'm trying to read it," Leila said, squinting closely. "Looks like a real amateur job, like maybe he did it himself."

"He probably did," Tusker said, imagining Uncle Chester killing time on deck of some Navy boat somewhere carving his name on his watch.

"*Sweetwater*," Leila said.

"Huh?"

"Yup, that's what it says," she said. "*Sweetwater*. Any idea what that means?"

Tusker thought for a while. "Well, it's only in English that we call the opposite of salt water 'fresh water.' Other languages translate it as sweetwater. Maybe it's a reference to the fact that he did a lot of diving in the Great Lakes." He shrugged.

Leila put the watch back in its pouch and then all the contents back in the box. It was too dark to see anything anymore and they rode in silence. The Scout's cabin was finally warm and the hum of the big tires hypnotic. Tusker rubbed his eyes and squinted ahead at the nearly empty road ahead. *Not much traffic heading north this time of day, or year,* he thought.

By the time they crossed the Mackinac Bridge onto the Upper Peninsula, Leila had fallen asleep. Tusker looked over at her smooth, angular face, lit by the green light from the instrument panel. Her mouth was open slightly and he had the urge to bend over and kiss her. He didn't notice the blue beams of the HID headlamps in his rearview mirror that had been following him ever since they left the cemetery.

Night Driving

Michigan Highway M-28.
The same day.

The state of Michigan has twice the shoreline mileage of California, bumping up against three of the five Great Lakes. The five-mile-long Mackinac Bridge connects the Lower and Upper Peninsulas, spanning the straits where Lake Michigan flows into Lake Huron. Once across it, the roads of the U.P. thin out and get more remote, passing by long, empty beaches and through dark forests, occasionally passing through small towns with French names like Brevort, Gros Cap, and Epoufette. These are some of the loneliest highways east of the Mississippi, and none more so than the Seney Stretch.

From the small town of Seney, due west to Shingleton, is a twenty-five mile, dead-straight stripe of highway that cuts through a desolate marshland. It is mind-numbingly dull, and typically empty save for the deer and occasional black bear that appear like a mirage, creating constant hazards. The road seems to go on forever and can lull a driver to sleep even in broad daylight. Every year there are a few deaths on the Seney Stretch, often attributed to inattention or animal strikes. Locals dread driving it, especially after dark.

As the Scout made the turn from highway 77 to 28 West at Seney, Tusker groaned to himself and sipped on the lukewarm coffee he'd picked up down in Mackinaw City. He struggled to keep his eyes open after driving for four hours. The Scout's headlamps were little help in the dark, casting two yellow cones of light that barely made it beyond the truck's front bumper.

Tusker had narrowly missed hitting a moose on the Seney Stretch years earlier, ending up in a roadside ditch up to his pickup's axles in snow. It took five hours for help to arrive. The memory of the experience made him wary. He backed off to around forty-five miles per hour. The old truck's brakes didn't inspire confidence. He glanced over at Leila, who was now leaning against the door, an old Pendleton blanket covering her shoulders, snoring softly.

When he looked back up at the road, he noticed the headlamps in his rearview mirror. They had been there earlier, but now were closer. He could tell by their wide set white pinpricks that it was a modern vehicle, probably an SUV. *Just pass me if you want,* Tusker thought, irritated. Some downstate tourist in a hurry, oblivious to what a deer could do to the windscreen of a car when hit at sixty-five. He slowed even further. The headlamps drew closer but didn't pass. Tusker put on his turn signal and pulled as far to the shoulder as he dared, then slowed even more. The headlamps were right on his bumper, not even visible in his mirror now.

"What the…" he shouted. Leila woke up just as they were struck. The impact caused the Scout to fishtail on the soft gravel shoulder and Tusker wrestled with the steering wheel.

"What's going on?" Leila shouted and swiveled in her seat, now wide awake. Tusker just grunted and got control of the Scout again, pressing the gas pedal to the floor to wake up the V8. The truck responded, lurching back on to the pavement and swerving into the oncoming lane before he straightened it out. *Was it a drunk driver?* Plenty of those up here, with all the small towns and taverns and long empty roads. *Or had the driver fallen asleep?*

As if in response, the vehicle closed the distance again, and Tusker heard the roar of a powerful engine as it bore down on them. He gritted his teeth and gripped the wheel, bracing for the impact.

"Hold on!" he shouted at Leila. She put her hands out and grabbed the top of the padded dashboard. The Scout took another blow and there was the sound of scraping metal. The truck was angled sideways and suddenly started to lean precariously. Tusker gunned the engine, and the Scout pulled free of the impact but was heading straight into the dark gully alongside the road. Leila screamed. The Scout careened off the gravel shoulder and pitched steeply, nose down, so that the headlamps showed only long grass that whipped past. Tusker jammed on the brakes. A tree loomed ahead and he jerked the wheel. At the last second they were past it, but then another tree came into view. The Scout grazed it and was spun around, finally coming to a stop. The engine had died, and the only noise was the ticking of it cooling off.

"Are you alright?" he leaned over to Leila, reaching out

for her face. She nodded, breathing hard.
"What happened?" she said, her voice trembling. Tusker hadn't seen her vulnerable before.

"Someone ran us off the road," he replied, looking over his shoulder. Through the rear window he could just make out the road and the red glow of taillights. "Stay here," he said firmly, and slid out of the truck. He could hear the guttural rumble of an engine idling. He crept along the gulley below the road and quietly climbed the wet grass to the gravel shoulder. Twenty yards further up the road, a vehicle was idling there, wisps of exhaust visible in the glow of the taillights. It was a large, dark colored SUV. A Suburban.

Tusker crouched low and crab walked up the shoulder, hoping he wouldn't be spotted. He instinctively reached in his pocket, then patted his leg for some sort of weapon. He swore to himself, remembering that he was wearing the black suit he'd put on for the funeral. He didn't have a plan, other than to stay out of sight until he reached the SUV. Though he had a pretty good idea who it was, he needed to be certain.

Just as he approached the passenger side of the Suburban and was reaching for the door handle, he heard a scream behind him. *Leila*. Tusker forgot about the Suburban, turned, and sprinted back to the Scout. He was running nearly blind in the darkness now. His leather soled brogues slid on the wet grass of the steep gulley, and he half fell, half scrambled down and across to where he could just make out the Scout. Stupid mistake, leaving Leila there. The driver of the Suburban had crept down to finish the job.

"Hey!" Tusker shouted. There was no point being stealthy now. He wanted to distract whoever it was from Leila. He could hear a commotion nearby, a car door slam, a woman shout. Then, Tusker was hit, hard, falling backwards on the grass. A heavy boot kicked him in the ribs. He grunted and rolled over to grab an ankle, but the attacker was gone. Moments later, he heard an engine rev and the sound of spitting gravel. Tusker got to his feet just in time to see the Suburban roar away down the highway. *Leila*. He turned and stumbled to the Scout, dreading what he might find.

"Are you OK?" A bright light blinded Tusker. It was Leila, holding up her iPhone's flashlight.

"Am I OK?" Tusker said incredulously. "What about you? I heard a scream."

"Someone tried to pull me out of the truck," she said. "I slammed his hand in the door. Actually, I think it might have been a woman, or else it was a man who screams like a woman." She smirked.

Tusker slumped on the bumper of the Scout. The adrenaline was draining away now, and he felt utterly exhausted. His chest hurt and he felt a sharp pain when he inhaled. "I think I've broken a rib or two," he said, holding his side.

"Let's have a look," Leila said. "Hold this." She handed him her phone and started unbuttoning his shirt and lifted his thermal undershirt. "Oh yeah, it's already bruising." Tusker looked down at his naked chest. An ugly red patch was blooming on his right abdomen.

"I'll be fine," he said. "Let's see about getting this truck back on the road." He started to stand up, then faltered, unsteady.

"I don't think we're going anywhere tonight," she said. "I've never been camping before. You can show me how." She gave a mischievous smile.

Growing up in the Midwest, it had been drilled into Tusker to be prepared to get stranded in winter — blankets, a first aid kit, some food — and Tusker kept enough gear in his truck for the odd bivouac. It was loaded in an old canvas gear duffel with the name Tusk stenciled on it. His father's Navy sea bag. The Scout's rear bench seat flipped up so that the load bed in back was just big enough to lie down. Tusker had to instruct Leila how to do this since his injury rendered him useless. Then they unfurled a foam Therma-rest camping pad and the Pendleton blanket for a makeshift bed.

Leila lowered the truck's tailgate and helped Tusker climb in, then shimmied up herself and pulled the gate shut. It wasn't comfortable by any means, but it was cozy. Tusker produced a small steel flask from the duffel. He unscrewed the cap and passed it to Leila. She took a long pull on it.

"Mmmm, burning tires," she said. "Laphroiag?"

"Close, Lagavulin," Tusker replied. "Peaty whiskies are always best drunk outdoors."

They passed the flask back and forth silently until it was empty. The whisky warmed Tusker's stomach and dulled the pain in his ribs. It was dark in the truck, and cold. Their breath had steamed the windows. Tusker's mind reeled, going over what had happened, what morning would bring, and what to do next. The glowing hands of his Seiko read nearly eleven, and it reminded him of another time, another place, stranded in the middle of nowhere with a woman. It had been just over a year since he was drifting off the coast of Sri Lanka with Samanthi after surfacing from a dive, unsure if they'd even survive the night.

"Where are you?" Leila broke the silence, as if reading his mind.

"At sea," he said, shaken from his thoughts. Leila leaned over in the dark and kissed him softly on the mouth. Tusker could taste the smoky sweetness of the whisky on her tongue. She didn't say anything, but her hand slid inside his shirt and rubbed his bare stomach. He winced when she brushed his ribs but didn't say anything. She kissed him harder, and he responded. Her hand went further down, and he felt her unbutton his pants, those silly suit pants he'd been wearing since that morning. He moaned as she touched him and then he reached under her sweater.

"Eek! Your hands are freezing!" She giggled and pushed his hands away, but without much resistance. He felt her small, firm breasts and the hard nipples. She got to her knees, so he saw her silhouette in the cramped back of the truck. She pulled the skirt above her waist and then swung a leg over Tusker's hips. It was warm there and she moved on him, slowly at first, then faster. Tusker arched his back, and pain overtook his pleasure.

"Ah!" he called out and recoiled. Leila froze, then laughed and rolled off him on to the camping pad. Tusker could hear her breath starting to slow. "I'm sorry," Tusker said. "My ribs..."

"No need to apologize," she said. Even in the dark he could tell she was smiling. "I can still do something to help relieve your pain."

Half an hour later, they lay quietly next to each other in silence. The sweat from their pleasure now brought a chill. Somewhere in the woods outside, an owl hooted. Tusker pulled the blanket up over them and beckoned Leila to come closer.

"I guess camping is fun after all," she said. "And here I thought it was all bugs and freeze-dried food."

Tusker laughed hard, then shouted in pain. "You made me forget about my broken ribs for a while there."

"Never let it be said that I don't care."

Raindrops started drumming on the roof of the Scout. The long November night was settling in. It was going to be a cold one.

The Schooner

Marquette, Michigan.
The next day.

The next morning, Carl arrived in a Dodge pickup he'd borrowed from the shipyard and towed the Scout back up onto the road. Then he followed Tusker and Leila as they limped into Marquette, the old truck pulling badly to one side, its muffler hanging off at an odd angle.

"Tusker knows how to show a girl a good time, doesn't he?" Carl said to Leila as they stood in the parking lot of the Landmark Inn. "Well, it was nice meeting you, despite the circumstances. Maybe next time, you should do the driving." He winked, then drove off.

Tusker spent that weekend with Leila in her hotel room. She brought him bags of ice for his ribs and went out to fetch Thai food in cardboard cartons and plenty of beer. They spent the two days napping, talking, and making love. Leila told him about her upbringing in Detroit with conservative Lebanese parents, her year traveling through South America, and an ill-fated short marriage to an abusive husband. Tusker recounted in kind, detailing his experiences in Sri Lanka, his recent panic attacks, and his fraught relationship with his father. Leila had asked about his relationship with Samanthi and showed no hint of jealousy when he told her.

"Yeah, it's good you're seeing this therapist," she said without a hint of sarcasm. It reminded Tusker that he needed to get another session scheduled with Dr. Fuchs for the following week.

On Monday, he dropped the Scout at a repair shop to correct its badly damaged steering and fix the muffler, then walked over to the clinic to get his ribs looked at. As he had expected, X-rays indeed showed two cracked ribs. "Take it easy for a few weeks," his doctor told him. "No lifting or hard exercise until those ribs heal."

Tusker picked up a prescription for painkillers and went back to the hotel. Leila was sitting on the bed wearing an oversized T-shirt and boxer shorts, typing on her laptop. She looked up and smiled when Tusker came in.

"I just submitted my story about Hockenheimer," she said. "My editor says they're fact checking it, and with any luck it'll run tomorrow, front page."

"If we thought he was pissed at us before, just wait til he reads that," Tusker replied, smiling.

"This is only the beginning," Leila said. "My hope is that it will bring more evidence out of the woodwork. If the senator is implicated in Overbrook's plane crash, it will be one of the biggest news stories of our generation."

Tusker popped the top of the prescription bottle, took two

pills out and swallowed them with a swig of coffee. He was happy for Leila, but something didn't sit right with him. Why hadn't his father processed that film? Why had he and Chester stayed quiet all those years if they knew something wasn't right about that crash?

While Leila went back to work on her laptop, Tusker opened his MacBook at the small desk in the corner of the room. He'd been ignoring his work e-mails and had taken the week off from teaching at Tech. His PhD students were mostly self-sufficient by this time, and he didn't teach his basic underwater course until the spring semester, so his workload was fairly light. But when he opened his inbox, the unread e-mails poured in. Most were spam, and some were related to his recent Jamaica project. He scanned the list for anything that needed attention. Near the top was one from a familiar name: the office of Senator Theodore Hockenheimer.

The e-mail was from some lower-level aide, written in a polite but terse manner, requesting a meeting with Mr. Julian Tusk that evening at 5:00 at a restaurant called The Schooner. Tusker was about to hit Reply when he noticed there was an attachment. He clicked to open it. It was a photograph, obviously scanned from an old 35 mm film image. In it, two men dressed in black diving suits, their faces painted in dark grease paint, were looking up from a small inflatable boat with serious expressions. Tusker recognized them. One was his father. The other was Chester Basch. He typed a terse reply, "I'll be there," then slammed his laptop shut.

For the rest of the day, Tusker was moody and withdrawn.

He didn't tell Leila about the e-mail or the meeting with Hockenheimer. At 4:30, he said he had to go pick up the Scout and left the Landmark. He walked to the shop and collected the truck. It still looked rough from being run off the road. The rear quarter was dented in. The shop had managed to fix the broken taillight and the muffler, but had left the dented metal with a smear of grey primer paint. At least the alignment had been corrected, thanks to a straightened steering rod. Tusker drove it slowly downtown, parking it near the ore dock, which loomed like a battleship in the darkness.

What did Hockenheimer know about his father? Tusker sat in the truck, staring out at the lake. At five, he got out, slammed the door and walked the two blocks up the hill to meet the senator.

The Schooner was a survivor from the days when Marquette was still a blue-collar industrial town, and little about it had changed since the 1970s. The illuminated sign over the door buzzed and blinked, one of the 'O's in its name burned out. There were two black SUVs parked outside, exhaust curling up from beneath them. Two broad-shouldered men in suits stood nearby, obviously part of Hockenheimer's security detail. Tusker opened the heavy, carved wooden door and pushed inside. It was dark and overheated and it took a while for his eyes to adjust. The only light seemed to come from red shaded lamps over the tables and the long bar. The walls were covered in old photos and nautical ephemera — ship's wheels, pennants, life rings. Though indoor smoking had been outlawed for years, it still smelled like an ashtray. Glasses clinking, a burst of laughter from the end of the bar, and two waitresses gossiping in the corner were the muted soundtrack to the scene. Only a couple of tables were occupied in the dining room, neither of which held Senator Hockenheimer.

"May I help you?" A plump hostess with too much makeup sauntered up as Tusker stood at the podium.

"I'm supposed to be meeting someone here," Tusker replied. "Ted Hockenheimer."

The hostess smiled. "You must be Julian," she said, fluttering her eyelashes coyly. "He's in the Commodore Room, honey. You can go right back."

She pointed to a closed door near the back of the bar. Tusker nodded and gave a small smile, then walked through the dining room, his shoes sticking to the dark red carpeting. Another heavy, dark wooden door, this one with a brass plaque over it that read "Commodore Room." Tusker started pushing it open, and someone on the other side pulled it wide. It was Slider, the bodyguard. She was dressed in her usual tactical getup, but her left hand was wrapped in some sort of bandage. For once she wasn't wearing her dark sunglasses, and Tusker noticed one of her eyes was glassy and pale, perhaps the result of an old injury. The other was black, showing no iris at all, and it bored into Tusker with undisguised malice.

"Car accident?" Tusker smiled gaily and gestured to her injury. She didn't reply.

"Slider, let our guest in," Hockenheimer's smooth voice

called from the far end of the room. Slider stood back a step and Tusker walked past.

"Charming staff you have," Tusker said as he approached the table where the senator was seated. It was a large table, big enough for a party of ten at least, but Hockenheimer was seated in the middle of a heavily padded banquette with studded red leather. Besides the bodyguard and a lone waiter, he was the only person in the room. The senator stood up and wiped his mouth with a white napkin and extended a hand across the table. Tusker shook it. The handshake was firm.

"A career of service comes with its unfortunate threats. It's a necessity to have close personal protection these days," Hockenheimer said. "Slider is a longtime trusted member of my team. She's a teddy bear once you get to know her." He grinned. Tusker smirked and sat down in a wooden chair opposite the senator.

"Fast roping, not baseball, in case you're wondering about her name," he continued. "Slider was part of a tactical intervention team in the Gulf when she served. Those pirates never stood a chance." The senator beamed like a proud father. "When she lost an eye during one raid, she was discharged, and I hired her. She sees more with one eye than most people do with two."

Tusker looked back at the menacing woman, who now stood in a dark corner watching him. The prosthetic eye caught a reflection and glowed eerily.

"You'll forgive me for starting to eat but I have to be in

Detroit to meet some supporters later tonight, so my time is a bit short. I catch a bite when I can," the senator continued.

Tusker nodded. He could see a half-eaten rare steak on the senator's plate, blood pooling around a blob of glutinous potatoes. "Please, order what you like." Hockenheimer waved and the waiter hustled over from across the room.

"Beer," Tusker said without looking up. "Stout if you've got one, and not too cold." The server disappeared. "So why did you want to see me privately, Senator? Worried your message wasn't getting through?"

Hockenheimer finished chewing a gristly piece of meat and chuckled, ignoring the comment. "I wanted to run an idea past you." He shifted in his seat, then lifted a glass of red wine to his lips and drank deeply from it. Tusker could see a large steel watch, a Breitling, slide down his wrist. It was a predictable symbol of machismo.

"I'm fully intending to be in the White House in January, and when I am, I want to raise the awareness and stature of our home region." He gestured to Tusker and himself. "The Great Lakes is one of America's greatest resources, and has, frankly, been undervalued by past administrations. We've been the breadbasket of the world, our iron has fed the steel mills, our ships have carried our products all over the world. And soon, our fresh water will be coveted all over the country."

"Spare me the campaign speech, Senator," Tusker said.

"And aren't you from New Jersey?"

The waiter set down a pint glass with a foamy molasses-dark liquid in it. Tusker nodded to him and took a sip, then wiped his lips.

"OK, I'll get right to it because I know you're more aware than most about all of this," the senator's tone turned serious, and he leaned his elbows on the table. "I'll need someone in my administration I can trust to lead our environmental initiatives, and I want Michigan, and the Great Lakes, at the center of those initiatives." Tusker could see what was coming. The senator continued.

"The EPA and NOAA have been ineffectual for too long. I want to fold the two under one level of oversight and I'd like you to be a part of this new organization. I don't have a title yet, but 'Freshwater Czar' has a nice ring to it, wouldn't you say?" He grinned widely and Tusker could see a stringy piece of sinew stuck between his teeth.

Tusker whistled and sat back in his chair. He took a sip of the stout and shook his head. "I'm not a politician, Senator, nor do I like office work," he said. "Anyway, what makes you think a professor of underwater archaeology is qualified? I explore shipwrecks for a living."

"I've seen your persistence and have heard about your level of commitment to causes you believe in, and your lifetime living and working in the Lakes is not something to be underestimated," Hockenheimer said.

"What's the catch here, Senator," Tusker said, getting impatient. He glanced at his watch. "Let's cut to the chase, shall we?"

"No catch. Just offering you a considerable bump in salary, a high position commensurate with your experience, and all I ask for is your loyalty."

"And my silence?" Tusker said. The senator's face went dark, and he gave a frustrated sigh.

"I know you and Ms. Mansour think you have some sort of scoop," he said, his tone less cordial. "But digging up history will serve no one well. Least of all, you." He fixed Tusker's eyes with his own and Tusker saw something new in them, a genuine malice.

"If you're hiding something, Senator, don't the voters deserve to know the truth?" Tusker shot back.

"And what is the truth, Mr. Tusk?"

"Oh, for example, how you got your Senate seat in the first place? I know that plane crash wasn't an accident, or pilot error." Tusker said. "My father knew the truth. So did Chester Basch. I don't know why they didn't say anything, but *I'm* not going to keep quiet."

The senator suddenly snapped his fingers and gestured. Tusker heard movement behind him. Slider approached and Tusker braced for anything—a blow to the back of the head, a gunshot. But the woman only handed a thick yellow envelope to Hockenheimer, then retreated.

"No need to be jumpy, Mr. Tusk," the senator said, once again calm and smiling. "I just think as long as you're pursuing 'the truth' as you call it, you might as well know the *whole* truth." He unwound the string that held the envelope shut and pulled out a sheaf of documents. He set the pile on the table and slid it across to Tusker. "Here, have a look," he said. "Of course, this doesn't leave this room, but take your time."

Tusker looked at the pile of papers in front of him warily, as if it would explode in his face. The cover sheet was titled, "United States Naval Investigative Service Report: Operation Steelfish, August, 1969." He flipped over the yellowed pages gingerly. As he read, he could hear Hockenheimer cutting meat, chewing noisily, then slurping wine, across the table.

The report, complete with sketched diagrams, black and white photographs, and mimeographed handwritten statements, detailed a covert operation during the Vietnam War involving the Underwater Demolition Team and a suspected Viet Cong sabotage attempt. As Tusker continued reading, he came across the photograph that had been attached to the e-mail earlier that day. Below it was the caption, "UDT divers Tusk and Basch." Tusker's skin went cold.

"I'm happy to tell you the short version if you'd rather not read the whole thing." Hockenheimer's voice broke the silence in the room. "And frankly, I need to, since I have a plane to catch." He sounded as smug as he did in the countless TV campaign ads Tusker had seen. Tusker didn't look up, but the senator continued.

"Your father, and his… friend, Basch, blew up a fishing trawler that was smuggling refugees fleeing from North Vietnam. Women, children… thirty-two people in total. Your father even managed to kill two men with his knife." He slid his hand across his throat for added effect. "They were brought before the NIS to answer for it."

Tusker's brain was reeling. He leaned closer to the pages, as if looking for something, anything that would disprove what the senator was saying. "But… I'm sure they were acting on intel. The UDT wasn't a commando unit. They followed orders…"

"They were specifically told to assess the threat posed by the fishing trawler. Clearly, they acted with extreme prejudice." Hockenheimer said, saying the last words slowly.

So this is what the senator had on his father and Chester. Tusker looked up at Hockenheimer finally. "You blackmailed them," he hissed.

Hockenheimer shook his head and wagged a finger. "The 'fog of war,' some called it. It was a complicated time. Soldiers and sailors didn't get the benefit of the doubt back then. People here in America spat on them, called them baby killers. I didn't want to see the reputations of two good Navy men get sullied. Basch was the first Black UDT man to receive the Bronze Star, did you know that?" Hockenheimer drained his wine glass. The waiter stepped forward, but Hockenheimer waved him away. He pressed on.

"At the time, I was a Lieutenant working for the NIS. When this report came across my desk, I saw an opportunity. An opportunity to right a wrong. Your father and Basch didn't deserve to be punished for killing a bunch of gook peasants."

Tusker glared at him. "So you buried the report," he said, smoldering. He wanted to reach across and stick the senator's own steak knife into his forehead. But then he thought about his father. It was starting to become clear to him why he was so withdrawn and never talked about the war, why he discouraged Tusker from joining the military, and why Chester had told him not to dig further into the plane crash.

"Let's just say, your father and I had a symbiotic relationship. And, as I said, digging up the past doesn't really serve anyone well. I'd hate to see how this report would tarnish the Tusk name, or the Basch name for that matter." He reached across the table and pulled the pile of papers back towards him, aligned the corners neatly, and slid them back into the envelope. Then he stood up, signaling the end of their meeting. Tusker stayed seated.

"I got a call from the *Detroit Free Press* this afternoon, asking me for a statement about Overbrook's plane crash. It seems your friend, Ms. Mansour, has been writing fairytales." Hockenheimer pulled a black overcoat on over his suit. "If the basis of her theory is the word of some… war criminal UDT divers, well, let's just say it might be best if she reconsiders her sources."

Hockenheimer patted Tusker on the shoulder as he

walked past. "Feel free to order some dinner on my tab, if you'd like. The steak is quite nice if you order it bloody." Tusker heard the door to the Commodore Room close behind him.

Operation Steelfish

Cam Ranh Bay, Vietnam.
August, 1969

The sixty-foot steel trawler had been seen offshore, moving up and down the coast for three days, always after dark. A P-2 Neptune patrol plane was tracking its movements, relaying its positions and aerial photographs to the MACV eggheads at Tan Son Nhut. Finally, word came down: Operation Steelfish was a go.

Jonathan Tusk wanted some action. He'd been sweating it out on board the amphibious transport submarine, USS *Grayback,* for a week. Unlike the regular crew of the sub, his four-member Underwater Demolition Team detachment had few day-to-day responsibilities until they got a mission. They spent their time lounging in the mess, playing cards, smoking, and sharpening their Ka-Bars. Many of the frogmen, as they'd become known, had let their hair get long and grown mustaches, so they more resembled peacenik hippies than enlisted sailors. "Big wristwatches and little peckers," the *Grayback* crew used to jealously chide them.

To stay fit and cool off, Tusk took to swimming off the sub's narrow deck, occasionally spearfishing when they were stationary, usually with no luck. He and Chester Basch had an ongoing arm-wrestling competition. Basch was winning.

"UDT platoon, report for briefing." The call had finally come. The frogmen assembled in the captain's cramped stateroom to get their orders. A nautical chart of Cam Ranh Bay was laid out on a table and a man in civilian clothes that Tusk didn't recognize was leaning over it. *CIA? MACV?* Tusk thought. *When did he come aboard?*

The captain cleared his throat to quiet the room. "Alright, guys, you've been asking for a mission and we've got one for you. This is Mr. Balesi from the Studies and Observations Group, who will outline the plan." He stepped back and the MACV-SOG man looked at the sweating faces around the room

"We've got a high degree of certainty that this trawler is VC," Balesi said, without any sort of greeting, pointing at a sheaf of black and white aerial photos splayed out on top of the chart. "Its proximity to our vessels in Cam Ranh Bay, and what we interpret as hostile intentions, necessitate its elimination. We're calling this Operation Steelfish."

These spooks and their euphemisms, Tusk thought. "How high a degree of certainty they're Viet Cong?" he asked, squinting at Balesi, whose short-sleeved dress shirt looked out of place on a warship.

"High enough," he replied, fixing Tusk with a stare. Tusk chuckled and shook his head. The man brushed a lock of hair away from a damp forehead and adjusted his glasses, then continued.

"From our analysis of their movements, the trawler should be passing across the south end of the mouth of the bay between 0300 and 0330 tomorrow." He looked around the room. "Our plan is to deploy two swimmers from an IBS ahead of the trawler's line of travel." IBS, the *Inflatable Boat, Small,* or "Itty Bitty Ship" as it was better known, was the UDT's primary mode of transport, essentially a blow-up dinghy with a small outboard motor.

"The swimmers will intercept the trawler, deploy limpets here and here," he continued, pointing to two X's on a sketch of the trawler's profile, "and then swim away and await pickup by the IBS for return to the *Grayback.* Fuses on the limpets should be set for no more than two minutes, which should leave ample time to move out of any blast zone."

"So let me get this straight." Basch moved to the front of the assembled group of UDTs, his fists pressed into his hips, leading with his imposing chest. "You want us to swim into the path of a moving boat?"

"The Neptune has tracked the speed of the trawler at no greater than two or three knots," the SOG man said, clearly uncomfortable with the confrontation. "We've calculated…"

"This is a suicide mission," Basch said, shaking his head, his voice raised. The other UDTs muttered their agreement. "And what happens if we are seen? Two swimmers against a boat full of Viet Cong?"

"You'll have to get wet," Balesi responded coldly, with a euphemism for shedding blood.

Basch was about to speak when Tusk spoke up. "The only way to make this work is if we position two of us far enough apart in the path of this boat, with a net between us. The bow will catch the net and pull us in towards opposite sides of her hull. We'll need to calculate the correct width of this net to put us at the right points on each side." He reached out and pulled a pen from Balesi's shirt pocket and sketched his plan on the trawler drawing. "We can use the net as something to hold on to while we attach the limpets."

"Sounds like you're volunteering," Balesi said to Tusk.

"If you can assure us your intel is solid, I'm game to try," Tusk replied. "Getting a bit bored roasting on this old tub anyway. No offense, Captain." He looked over at the *Grayback's* captain, who nodded back.

Chester Basch sighed. "Can't let Tusk get all the glory. I'm in too."

At two thirty the following morning, Tusk, Basch, and the other two frogmen were perched on the flat, narrow deck of the *Grayback*, sitting high and dry in the IBS. A line was secured to the sub's periscope. They were wearing rubber diving suits despite the clammy tropical heat, and had smeared black greasepaint on their faces, which glistened in the light of the three-quarter moon. Each had a deflated buoyancy vest around his neck, and a heavy limpet mine clipped to a sling, worn bandolier style across their chests. Basch also had a tightly bundled nylon net that they had cut and reinforced in the supply room of the ship the night before. They both wore their Ka-Bar knives on their belts.

The SOG man had gone as quickly as he'd arrived, without a word of "good luck" or "farewell," probably back to his air-conditioned office in Saigon or at Ton Son Nhut Airbase. Tusk had heard an outboard motor at dusk.

The frogmen in the inflatable boat looked silently at each other and then synchronized the time on their dive watches, ensuring the crowns were screwed in. Then they waited. At two-forty-five, the submarine began to disappear beneath them, slowly submerging below the water's surface. The dinghy remained floating, its bow line still attached to the sub's periscope. The sub began to arc towards the headland at the south end of the Cam Ranh Bay. There were no other boats visible, and the water had an oily black sheen.

None of the frogmen spoke during the twenty minute ride to the rendezvous spot. Tusk pulled back his dive suit sleeve and squinted at his watch. The luminous markers showed close to three. One of the other UDT men nodded and released the tow line. The boat coasted to a stop. Basch blew puffs of air into a tube on his buoyancy vest. It wouldn't be much, but would help him stay afloat with the heavy mine and net until the trawler came. Tusk did the same. With some shared hand signals, both men slid silently into the water, each taking an end of the net. The two other UDT men paddled the small boat away into the darkness.

As they'd planned earlier, Tusk would swim west, unspooling the net as he went, while Basch would tread water in place until it went taut. Tusk started an efficient combat swimmer's stroke, clutching the corner of the net in his hand. Every ten strokes, he paused and consulted his wrist compass. When the net went tight, he stopped swimming and bobbed in the water, allowing the weighted corner of the net to fall free. He clipped the other corner to his bandolier webbing. Then, they waited.

After what seemed like an eternity, Tusk heard the slow chug of an ill-tuned diesel engine. He followed the sound, and after a few minutes, the shape of a large boat appeared, silhouetted against the night sky. His watch read 3:40am. Would their position be correct? The Neptune had plotted a nightly course that was nearly identical for a week, but only a few yards off and they'd have missed the boat entirely. It drew closer. Tusk could hear muted voices carrying across the water. Vietnamese voices. The boat didn't have lights.

Suddenly it loomed above him. Chester would be a hundred feet away from him, at the other end of the net. If their position was correct, the bow would snag the net in its center and pull both men in, fifty feet back on each side of the boat's hull. Tusk started to release air from the buoyancy vest by pulling its vent cord. He sunk lower in the water so that only his head was above the waves. They'd not worn diving masks to avoid the risk of a reflection. He kicked hard against the weight of the mine that wanted to pull him under. Salt water stung his eyes.

Finally, a hard tug. The bow had caught. Tusk and Basch were dragged along by the trawler. It might have only been doing two or three knots, but it was hard to hold on, and Tusk's head kept being pulled under the water. Finally, he came alongside the hull. He quickly maneuvered the mine so that its powerful magnet gripped the side of the steel boat. With it clipped to his harness, he was able to rest briefly and catch his breath.

The sideboard of the trawler was lower than he'd imagined. Whatever its use now, it was originally a fishing vessel, built for hauling nets and lines aboard from the sides. Tusk could hear voices just a few feet above his head. Two men on board were laughing at some joke told in Vietnamese. *No attempt at being quiet,* Tusk thought. He smelled cigarette smoke and the overpowering odor of rotting fish. What if this wasn't Viet Cong? MACV had gotten things wrong before. He dismissed the doubts. His job was operational, not to question decisions in the field. No doubt Basch was almost done positioning his limpet on the other side of the boat.

Tusk unclipped the net from his harness and it fell away into the sea. All that held him to the ship now was the limpet. He had marked the two minute fuse timer with a dot of phosphorus paint and he set it, then spun the bezel on his dive watch to sync it. Then, he unclipped the mine from his harness and prepared to drop away into the water. Suddenly there was a cacophony of voices above him, and he felt himself lifted away from the hull, suspended briefly in midair, held by his arms.

Tusk was dragged on board and tossed to the deck. In the darkness, he could see he was surrounded by a circle of men, their faces indistinguishable. Several were shouting at him in Vietnamese. He heard the word "American." This was it. Killed or rotting in an NVA prison camp was not in his plans. He unsheathed his knife and lunged at the closest man. He felt the blade get purchase and heard a groan. He pulled back, then slashed at the next man. A gurgle. Now his attackers were wary, backing away. Where were their weapons? If this was a Viet Cong boat, he expected everyone to be aiming an AK-47 at him by now. But they were frozen in place. The two men he'd stabbed lay motionless on the deck, dark pools of their blood mingling.

Tusk had to get off this boat. He looked at his wrist to check the limpet's fuse timer, but his watch was gone, probably ripped off his wrist when they'd pulled him on board. Basch would be floating somewhere well in their wake by now. With one swift move, Tusk sheathed his knife, turned, and jumped over the side into the black bay. The boat churned past him, and he swam away from it to keep from being pulled into its propellers. As he did, he heard a distinctive sound, out of place in the middle of a dark sea, in the middle of the night, in the middle of a war: a baby crying. Then a woman's voice, the familiar plaintive tone of a mother comforting an infant. It faded away with the boat into the darkness.

Twenty seconds later, the trawler exploded.

Burn It All

Lac La Belle.
Present day.

Tusker sat on the floor near the wood stove, shoving papers in and watching the flames consume them. Most of it was old bills, receipts, a calendar from 1987, the Houghton phone directory, and a few letters. The cabin was still a mess. He hadn't cleaned up after the break-in, but merely pushed piles of debris enough to walk through. Now he just wanted to burn the whole place down.

Earlier that night, after leaving The Schooner, he had gone back to the Landmark Inn and told Leila about his meeting with Hockenheimer. He told her about his father and Chester, Operation Steelfish, and the senator's thinly veiled threat. Then he asked her to pull her story.

"No way!" she said angrily. "This is the biggest story of my career. Hell, it'd be the biggest story of anyone's career, and it's only going to get bigger."

"All I'm asking is that you wait a few more days, just until I have a chance to look into things further." Tusker was trying to calm her down.

"The election is in a week!" A vein stood out in stark relief on her forehead. "There aren't a 'few more days.' This man is dangerous, and he could very well be our next president! People need to know about this. I'm sorry, but it's way more important than your dad's legacy."

"It's not about Dad's legacy," Tusker said, getting exasperated. "I'm just saying, it will be a much stronger story if we can piece together a few more clues, like Hockenheimer's blackmail, the truth about the crash instead of just rumors… and who actually shot down the plane. Did you even think about that detail?"

She shot him a look. "Don't patronize me. I know how to build a story and what I submitted isn't the whole one. It's only the beginning. It rattles Hockenheimer's cage, makes other people come forward, forces him to answer some tough questions."

"Just give me two more days then, please," he cajoled. "That's all I ask. I'll get you more evidence, I promise. You can run the story without it if I fail. Just two more days."

In the end, he wasn't sure she would give in. She didn't say anything after that, but instead grabbed her leather jacket and motorcycle helmet and stormed out of the room. It was implied that she didn't want him to be there when she came back. He drove the Scout back to Lac La Belle and the cold, dark cabin.

Now he sat by the roaring fire with a half-drunk bottle of Talisker and the pack of Camels he'd bought at a gas station on the way home. The cigarettes made him cough and it hurt his ribs. He washed down two more Vicodin with a mouthful of the Scotch. As he reached for more detritus to burn, he saw the small box Lydia Basch had given him at the funeral. *Basher. So he was in on it too.*

He poured another two fingers of Talisker and pulled the box closer, then opened it. He took out the Tudor watch and studied it. It looked like it had been through the wars—at least one of them. Tusker turned it over and squinted at the engraving on the back—Sweetwater. The scratching didn't appear as old as the dings and marks on the rest of the watch case. Its crude lines caught the light from the fire and glinted. It was as if Chester had carved it there recently. He set it aside and pulled out the rest of the box's contents.

It was an odd mish-mash of papers, mostly newspaper clippings, and none seemed to relate to Tusker or his father. He wondered why Chester had wanted him to have them. He was about to toss them in the wood stove when one clipping caught his eye. It was from the *Navy Times*, a paper published biweekly for active and retired members of the U.S. Navy. The article was titled, "Members of Pacific Fleet Meet Soviet Counterparts." Tusker scanned the article. Some Cold War effort at easing tensions, staged over a dinner on board an historic destroyer docked in Long Beach. But it was the photo that caught Tusker's eye. Yes, there he was: Lieutenant Theodore Hockenheimer, standing next to a Soviet naval officer, both shaking hands and grinning. Tusker set it aside.

Another clipping was a yellowed, torn page from the

Munising Weekly Miner. It was dated November 4, 1978 and titled, "Eyewitness Describes Flash in the Sky Before Plane Crash." A local fisherman named Tom Bouchet had been returning to Munising from a late season run for lake trout when he saw what he described as, "a streak of light, followed by what looked like fireworks." He hadn't even realized there was a plane crash until he watched the news the next morning. Tusker laid it gently on top of the *Navy Times* clipping.

After rummaging through a few more clippings in the box, Tusker came to the last one. It didn't seem to fit with the rest. It looked like one of those community human-interest stories small town papers run from time to time. It had a black and white photo of a middle-aged, heavy-set man with bristly gray hair and an unruly beard. He was wearing an apron, standing in front of what looked like a bakery case. He was smiling, holding a tray with some sort of pastry on it. "Russian Immigrant Opens Pastry Shop in Big Bay." How did this one relate? Maybe it was simply put in the bottom to line the cardboard box. Tusker was about to throw it in the fire when he saw something that made his skin go cold. On the man's apron was embroidered the name of his shop: "Sweetwater Pirozhkis."

The Largest Lake in the World

Lake Baikal, Russia.
Summer, 1969.

There are two largest freshwater lakes in the world. Lake Superior holds the claim for its vast surface area, large enough that if the country of Sri Lanka were dropped into it, it would still be an island, with room to spare. Ireland would come close with just a bit of overlap. Then there is Lake Baikal, in southern Siberia. Though smaller than Superior, on the surface, it has a maximum depth of 5,300 feet and a volume equal to all of the Great Lakes combined.

Yuri Sokolov learned these facts as a small boy growing up on the shores of Baikal, in a town so small it didn't even have a name. It was a point of pride for those who lived on the lake, and for most Russians, that it held more "sweet water" than any other lake in the world. From the humble wooden house his grandfather had built after the Revolution, Yuri could see through the thick pines and just make out the shimmer of the lake on long summer days. He walked its shores, learned to fish for pike and sturgeon from a rowboat, and, in winter, played hockey on its frozen surface with other village boys.

Yuri didn't know exactly what his father did for a living. Something connected with the gulag, the prison camp for enemies of the Revolution that was an hour's drive inland from the lake, deep in the forest. Dada was often gone for weeks at a time, always coming home with a big smile and gifts for Yuri and his mother — automaton toys from East Germany, itchy sweaters from Czechoslovakia, and fragrant loaves of rye bread.

During his father's long absences, young Yuri kept much to himself, poring over books, setting snares in the woods, and helping his mother in the kitchen. He loved rolling out the soft dough for her *pirozhkis*, the baked pastries she made, filled with cabbage, potato or the meat from a rabbit if he got lucky with a snare. The house had a record player, and when his mother wasn't playing her Tchaikovsky or bootlegged Elvis Presley LPs, Yuri would put on a scratchy record of English language lessons. The language fascinated him with its long, flat vowels and odd alphabet. He played both sides over and over and became proficient enough to say hello, ask for directions, and order in a restaurant. Of course, in Baikalia, he had no opportunity to practice, so he would make his mother laugh, speaking to her in an affected American accent, ordering coffee and asking how to get to the post office.

When he was home, Yuri's father taught his son how to shoot a gun, gut a deer, and drive the old Moskvitch up and down their dirt track. Yuri relished this time with Dada, soon forgetting the resentment he felt when he was gone. It was a paradise for a teenaged boy, and Yuri knew little about the outside world. He didn't need to. He had everything to make him happy right there on the remote shore of the big lake.

One summer night when Yuri was sixteen, his father arrived in a black GAZ sedan with another man, who told Yuri to call him Uncle Vlad. He smiled a lot but didn't talk much. He produced a bottle of crystal clear vodka and over a dinner of venison, boiled potatoes and blood red beets, Uncle Vlad and Dada downed glass after glass, their laughter carrying into the dark night. Uncle Vlad beckoned Yuri to join them, so he did. Yuri wasn't accustomed to drinking alcohol, and the vodka burned his throat and made his head feel funny. Vlad and Dada laughed at this and gave him more.

"Uncle Vlad has an important job for you, Yuri," Dada told him as they sat at the heavy wood table. Mama stood quietly at the sink washing dishes, listening. "He's going to take you with him tomorrow to the big city, to Moscow."

Yuri was crestfallen. He didn't want to leave, but he also didn't want to disappoint his father. Uncle Vlad, his cheeks red from drink, beamed down at Yuri.

"Your father has told me all about your skills, Yuri," he said, then belched loudly. "Your hunting, your driving, your English…"

Yuri blushed and stammered.

"It's OK, son," Dada said. "Your language practice will serve you well. You will be doing valuable work for Mother Russia."

When dawn broke the next day, the mist lingered on the lake. Loons wailed their mournful cry to each other and a lone owl hooted. Yuri's mother's face was swollen and wet with tears as she hugged him on the gravel driveway. His small vinyl suitcase was already in the GAZ's trunk and Uncle Vlad was in the driver's seat, engine running. The rich smell of exhaust soured the crisp morning air. Yuri's father opened the passenger door and put a hand on Yuri's shoulder.

"You'll make me proud, son," he smiled. "One day you'll make me proud."

Yuri looked past him at the lake. The first glitter of the sunrise danced off the surface of the water.

As the GAZ trundled down the drive and turned on to the dirt road, Yuri craned his neck and watched as his mother and father waved from the house. His mother was crying openly now. Beyond them, he saw Lake Baikal for the last time in his life.

Yuri hated Moscow. The city was grey and dirty in all seasons, crowded and unfriendly. For the next five years he lived in a comfortable but anonymous room in a windowless building near Gorky Park with a small group of other teenaged boys and girls. The ambiguous sign over the entrance read "Revolutionary Youth Education Ministry." There they spent mornings exercising in the cavernous gymnasium or running laps around the park, then the afternoon in classrooms, studying English language, American culture, and specific vocational skills such as carpentry or auto mechanics. The students were encouraged to interact and be friendly with each other, but outright friendships were discouraged.

One day, shortly after he turned seventeen, Yuri was summoned to a new wing of the ministry and told to wait in a room that had a large mirror on one wall and a small bed against the other. The door opened and a girl about his own age, but of Chinese or Mongolian appearance, was sent in. She seemed unsure of herself, and they both stood awkwardly, awaiting some sort of instruction. Finally, an older woman with pendulous breasts and heavy makeup came in. She sat on the bed and casually lit a cigarette, then told Yuri and the girl to take their clothes off. When they hesitated, the woman cackled. After they finally complied, she guided the two of them through various sexual positions and arousal techniques, including oral sex. Yuri had the feeling they were being watched through the mirror. The girl cried. Yuri hated it. It became a weekly part of their coursework, in what the students came to know as the *kompromat* class, and sex became as mechanical and routine as any of their other curriculum.

Also once a week, a small group of students were taken by bus an hour outside the city to an abandoned military camp. There they were taught how to strip, load, and fire a variety of guns, from Russian Makarovs to German Walthers, to American Colt revolvers. This was the only course Yuri enjoyed and he excelled at it. He earned a top rank among his classmates for marksmanship and was soon sent, with a smaller group, to another part of the camp, where he graduated to larger weapons and targets — grenade launchers, limpet mines, mortars, even surface-to-air missiles. Derelict cars were targets, first stationary, then some driven erratically around a field by terrified men who Yuri was told were enemies of the Revolution. He was told to eliminate them, and he did, at first hesitantly, then with a growing enthusiasm.

After five years at the Revolutionary Youth Education Ministry, Yuri was nothing like the boy who'd arrived from the shores of Lake Baikal. He could expertly fire any number of weapons, run a mile in five minutes, make a woman orgasm, and speak English with a perfect American accent.

One day, a familiar face appeared in the cafeteria while Yuri was eating his breakfast. It was Uncle Vlad. He greeted Yuri warmly.

"I've been following your progress closely," he said, patting him on the shoulder. "And I am told you are now ready to serve your country."

Yuri briefly considered asking about his parents, but didn't. He didn't really care anymore. He looked blankly at Vlad and nodded without emotion. "What is required of me, Comrade?" he asked.

"You are to go to America, Yuri. Settle down and live a normal and pleasant life—as normal and pleasant as you can in a decadent and corrupt capitalist country. Then, when the time is right, we will get word to you, and you will carry out your destiny."

Yuri perked up at the thought of America.

He remembered the English lessons on the record, Elvis, the books he'd read with images of wide open spaces, big cars, and gleaming cities. "Where will I be going in America, Comrade?"

"We have a special place for you there, Yuri. One we think you will like. It's much like your home in Baikalia." Uncle Vlad beamed, barely able to contain his excitement. "You are going to a place called Michigan."

The Recruit

Okinawa, Japan.
June, 1974

Looking back, the girl had seemed a little too compliant, too eager. He'd been with plenty of prostitutes off base during his year and a half posting on Okinawa. There had even been his "regular" girl, Mari, the one who teased that if he married her, she'd keep him hard and happy for the rest of his life. As if that would ever happen. He had a bright future ahead of him, one that didn't involve the complication of a Japanese bride. Still, he enjoyed her company, a rare bonus on top of the physical pleasures at which she was so adept. But then she disappeared, and he wondered if she'd found another officer who would give her a green card and live hornily ever after.

This new girl was different. She didn't speak English. He wasn't sure she spoke at all. She didn't need to. She was tall, a lot taller than the average Japanese woman, if she even was Japanese. He never did learn her name. She wore a blonde wig and bright red lipstick, and this excited him. She let him have his way, and he explored his own depraved fantasies in ways American girls would never let him. Now the memory of that evening in the cheap rented room above the noodle shop, brought back in vivid Kodachrome prints, made him sick.

"No one need ever know about this," the man with the thin mustache said, sliding the pile of photos back towards him, aligning their corners neatly, then tucking them into the inside pocket of his cheap suit jacket. He smiled briefly, then put a cigarette to his lips and lit it. He held out the pack, but the Navy man shook his head. They sat in a corner of the noodle shop. He'd sat at the exact table where he would wait for the girl. But this pale man with the mustache came instead.

"We know you have bigger aspirations, Lieutenant," the man said. "You are destined for great heights. All I want… all we want, is to help you achieve them."

"In exchange for what?" the man finally replied, his voice quavering. "I know you're a spy, but my knowledge of top secret military information is limited. I've been more focused on getting troops out of Vietnam the past year here."

The man across the table stubbed out the cigarette and took his time responding. "We take the long view, Lieutenant. Vietnam is not our concern. Our comrades in Hanoi have seen to that." The quick smile again. "And it's not your military career we care about. You are a rising star in America, our people there tell us. Your father has been grooming you for bigger things—politics, Congress… We can help you rise a little higher perhaps. All we would want in return is your… friendship."

"And the photos?"

"They will never be seen."

The officer looked around the noodle shop nervously. There were only a handful of people at other tables, all Japanese, all eating and talking. Sometimes servicemen came here for a bowl of udon and cheap saké, many of them also utilizing the rooms upstairs, with the girls who offered themselves outside.

"What do I need to do?" the officer finally said, glancing at his wristwatch.

"The beauty of this arrangement is, nothing at all. You simply proceed with your career and forget about any of this unpleasantness." He patted the chest of his suitcoat. "We will help you where we can, but you may never even know we are doing it. And when we do need you to repay our favor, we will contact you."

The lieutenant tensed his jaw and stared at the man across the table, who pulled another cigarette out and put it to his lips. The flare of his lighter came between them.

"You know I cannot betray my country," the Navy man said. "Those pictures could be of anyone. It was dark, the photos are blurry. No one will believe you."

The Russian shook his head, as if disappointed. He nodded ever so slightly to the cook behind the counter, a stocky Japanese man who was there every day serving bowls of steaming noodles to countless customers. He hurried over to the table and produced a small, flat box from his stained apron and set it on the table. The Russian nodded and the cook hustled away without a word.

"I'd hoped we wouldn't have to resort to this, Lieutenant." He lifted the lid off of the box, revealing a reel of film. The lieutenant banged his fist on the table, loud enough that the other diners looked over at him.

"It seems that your girl, Mari, was actually *our* girl, Mari," he wrinkled up his face in mock pain, shaking his head disapprovingly. "She was most cooperative… until she wasn't. It seems she fell for you." He took a long pull on his cigarette and exhaled a dramatic plume of smoke.

"You commie bastard!"

"It's nothing personal, Lieutenant. Our countries are engaged in a chess game and we use all the pieces at our disposal, just as your government does. You are merely a pawn." He used his cigarette to point to the lieutenant. "But a pawn who one day may become a king." The thin smile grew into a full grin, displaying gold capped teeth.

"Fine, I'll do what you ask," the officer replied. "But my family never gets touched, and if this all goes south, you pull me out. I'm not going to be hanged for treason!" He hissed the last word in a whisper.

The Russian nodded as he stubbed out the cigarette in the overflowing ashtray and pushed back his chair. He stood, placed a cheap fedora on his head, then bent over the table.

"It's not all bad, Lieutenant. Play by our rules and you

will, one day, be... how do they say? 'The leader of the free world.' That can't be all bad." He tucked the film box into the pocket of his trench coat, nodded to the cook, and strode to the door. As he did, two other men at another table— Japanese men— followed him out.

The lieutenant got up from his table, a bit dazed, and turned to go. As he did, the cook grinned at him from behind the counter. Outside the noodle shop, it had started to rain, the beginning of yet another tropical deluge. He didn't bother to hurry, or turn up his collar, but merely walked slowly back towards the base.

Closed for Business

Big Bay, Michigan.
Present day.

Big Bay, Michigan is best known for having been the setting and filming location of the 1958 film *Anatomy of a Murder*, starring James Stewart. In the film, Stewart plays a cocky lawyer who is asked to represent an Army lieutenant accused of murder. In his defense, the lieutenant claims the victim, a local innkeeper, had raped his wife, and that he has no recollection of the murder. The film was actually based on a true story, one that occurred in Big Bay.

Besides that faded claim to fame, and for having been the vacation getaway of Henry Ford, Big Bay is a quiet community of three hundred residents with a pretty lighthouse, views over Lake Superior, and a smattering of vacation cabins and small businesses that cater to summer tourists. There is a kayak outfitter, some kitschy souvenir shops, a tavern with a pretty good fish fry, the Lighthouse Bed and Breakfast where the movie was filmed, and, a mile or so along the shore, on a little-used county highway, a pastry shop.

The food and culture of the Upper Peninsula reflects its

history as a destination for waves of immigrants. The Cornish pasty, a baked hand pie typically filled with some sort of meat, was brought over by miners from Cornwall as something to eat during long days underground mining for copper. The fishing culture and cuisine came with Norwegians. And the pierogi, that filled dumpling that goes by many names, was proudly brought by Eastern European immigrants, from Poland, Hungary and Czechoslovakia. In Russian, this is called a pirozhki.

To Yuri Sokolov, the U.P. reminded him of home: the way the pine forest smelled on a hot summer day, the icy breeze off the big lake, and the feet of snow that buried the earth from November until May. He'd settled there in 1970, first finding work at the ore dock in Marquette, shoveling taconite pellets down in the holds of the big freighters that came calling. When the steel industry fell on hard times, he found odd work at a lumber mill, as a part-time hand on a fishing boat, and finally, with enough money in his pocket, he bought a derelict old general store outside of Big Bay and turned it into Sweetwater Pirozhkis. Business was good enough to sustain him, and he lived in a small apartment at the back of the bakery, keeping to himself, besides allowing a small local paper to write a story about his shop, which brought a modest bump in business.

From November through April, he was only open a few hours during the middle of the day, and sometimes had no customers. He kept the par-baked pirozhkis on sheet pans in a cooler, and baked them to order if someone came in. Otherwise, on less busy days, he was content to listen to his collection of vinyl records, read books, and look at the lake, which was visible through the trees out the back window of his apartment.

It was that kind of day when Tusker drove down the frost-tortured, potholed asphalt road and pulled the Scout into the gravel lot in front of Sweetwater Pirozhkis. There were no other vehicles there, other than an ancient Ford Gran Torino station wagon parked alongside the building, covered in a layer of dead leaves. Tusker peered through the Scout's windshield at the shop. It didn't look open. There were no signs of life and the windows were fogged over. There was nothing to indicate open or closed and the sign above the door wasn't illuminated. He shut off the engine and climbed down, hoping his four-hour drive hadn't been a wasted effort.

He approached the door, an aluminum one with a mesh cage over the outside of the glass and a full shade drawn down on the inside. He tried it. It swung open with a loud creak. The heavier inner door pushed inwards, triggering a bell that hung above it. He didn't see anyone at first, but heard music from somewhere in back, classical something or other.

"Hello?" Tusker called out. No answer. He leaned over the glass bakery case, which was empty, and tried to look down the hallway, from where the music was emanating. There was a bell on the countertop, and he gave it two sharp taps. It rang out. The music stopped. Tusker heard footsteps. A burly, older man appeared, the size of a small bear, with a bushy gray beard and a head of wild, unkempt hair. The man was wearing a quilted flannel shirt with a plaid pattern, faded Carhartt pants and an apron tied around his waist. He wiped his hands on it as he stepped up behind the counter.

"I'm afraid I don't have any pirozhkis today," he said, in a deadpan, unfriendly tone. "This time of year, I don't stay open much. Not much business." He had a slight accent that Tusker would not have been able to trace if it hadn't been for the newspaper clipping he'd read. Russian. It was definitely Yuri Sokolov, the man he'd seen in the photo—the same beard and hair, ursine heft—just older.

"In fact, you're lucky you caught me," the man continued. "I was about to lock up for the day. Not worth staying open."

Tusker smiled, trying to be pleasant. "I sure am lucky. But I wonder if you could make an exception and scare up something for me. I drove all the way from the Keweenaw. Even a cup of coffee would be great."

The man shook his massive head. "Sorry, I am about to close. I'm sorry that you made the long journey for nothing." He gestured to the door, dismissing Tusker.

Tusker changed tactics. "OK, I'll leave, but before I do, I'd like to ask you about the night of November 8th, 1978."

He detected the slightest change in the man's face, the corners of his mouth twitched down, his eyes darted to a corner of the room.

"I don't know that date. Was a long time ago. You must go now."

"I know about the airplane," Tusker said, taking a leap. It was a desperate maneuver, a gamble, and he held his breath to see if it would pay off. The man glared at him. Tusker could see his barrel chest heaving under the flannel shirt.

"I don't know what you're talking about. Now go!" Spittle flecked on to his beard as he spat the words. Just as he started to move out from behind the counter, there was the sound of a vehicle outside, gravel crunching. Tusker stepped quickly to the window and wiped a small circle of moisture from it. Through the smear, he saw a black Suburban idling outside, parked across the back of his Scout, as if to block an escape. He turned to the Russian.

"OK, look, I know the whole story, or at least I think I do, but there's no time to discuss it now. Ted Hockenheimer has sent someone to kill me," he was up close to the Russian now, in his face, whispering loudly. "And probably you too. You're the last witness to know the truth about what happened in '78. You and I are the only ones who could expose him and keep him from becoming president!"

Yuri hesitated, as if paralyzed. Deep down, he knew this day would come eventually. He knew it from the moment he fired the Strela at the Gulfstream. It had taken more than 40 years but here it was. The door opened, the bell clanging loudly with a cheerfulness that belied the tension in the room. Tusker turned.

Slider stood in the doorway, feet spread shoulder width apart, hands at her sides, like some kind of gunslinger in a Western. Her prosthetic eye glinted in the dull afternoon light. There was no pretending what this was about, no sneaking around in the cabin at night, or on a dark rural highway. A smile slowly appeared on the woman's face, like a zipper opening, revealing a row of white teeth. At the same moment, her right arm slowly but smoothly moved up and inside her Kevlar jacket.

Tusker reacted instinctively. Crouching low, he arched forward towards the towering woman, like a linebacker going for a tackle, and caught her squarely at the thighs with his shoulder. As he did, he felt a knee come up. It plowed into his side, into his already shattered ribs. He howled in pain and fell to the floor below her. A heavy boot stomped on his hand, but he managed to pull away so that she only caught two of his fingers. He rolled away, in a mist of pain. Had to ignore that now. She had a gun. This would be it.

Tusker spun to his feet and charged again, remembering that her left arm was injured, both where he'd slashed her with his knife at the cabin and where Leila had slammed her hand in the Scout's door. He aimed for it, hitting hard with all his weight. He gripped her wrist and twisted. Slider screamed, a guttural, piercing wail. She recoiled, knocking over the lone small table in the corner of the bakery. Tusker charged in again. He had her on her heels now. Again, the left arm was his target, her weak spot. He made his approach from that side, hoping the prosthetic eye would compromise her peripheral vision. But clearly it didn't, and as he moved in, she threw a classic boxing uppercut that caught him again in the ribs.

Tusker saw stars, gasping for breath. His vision was narrowing from the pain. *Don't. Black out. Now.* He reeled away, stumbling across what? A chair, a spindly wooden thing. It clattered to the floor, with Tusker's legs tangled in the chair's. Somehow, he kept his balance and managed to pick up the chair. It was a light pine kitchen chair, and he pivoted and, in a single motion, almost blindly aiming, swung it with all his strength. He heard a crack and a low grunt. Slider was on her knees. Tusker saw blood pouring from a cut above her left eye. He raised the chair again, but as he did, she leveled a sleek, black automatic pistol at him. Tusker stopped. Slider grinned. So this was it, he thought. This is how I die. He closed his eyes. Then, the deafening roar of a gun.

It took a moment for Tusker to realize he wasn't shot. When he opened his eyes, he saw Slider lying motionless on the checkered tile floor. A dark pool of blood already radiated from her head. Her eyes stared vacantly at the ceiling. Then Tusker realized what had happened. He looked across the bakery. There was Yuri, standing in his flannel shirt and apron, holding a black Makarov pistol, smoke still wisping from its barrel.

Tusker crumpled to the floor.

Vodka for Dinner

Big Bay, Michigan.
The same day.

The smell woke him up. Food. Something baking. Tusker opened his eyes, and it took a few seconds to register where he was. The room was dark, but a dim shaft of light appeared under a door at the far end. He was lying on a scratchy sofa, with a lumpy pillow under his head. He tried to sit up, and as he did, a stab of pain in his chest caused him to shout. He rolled to the floor on his knees and hunched in a ball of agony. Slowly, he uncoiled and eased back on to the sofa.

His eyes adjusted to the dark now, and he scanned the room. It was almost too much to take in, indistinct shapes, floor to ceiling bookshelves crammed with countless objects: boxes and books and clothes and coffee mugs and bottles on every horizontal surface. A big window on one wall was covered by heavy curtains so there was no sense of day or night. He looked at his watch's faintly glowing hands — 6:15. Evening, had to be. He'd been out for hours. Suddenly he remembered something and fumbled for his phone, which had been wedged in his back pants pocket. The screen lit up, burning into his retinas. It had a new jagged crack across the screen, but it still worked.

Seven missed calls and as many text messages.

Ignoring them for now, he navigated to the homepage of the *Detroit Free Press*, holding his breath. A new mass shooting was the lead story. He scrolled. The Lions lost again. Further down, an endorsement by the paper's editorial board of Hockenheimer for president. But nothing about the plane crash investigation. Leila had held the article. He exhaled, then read through the missed messages. All were from Leila. He quickly typed a reply: "I'm OK. Found the Russian. Will have something for you soon. Don't call." He set the phone down. Footsteps approached outside the door.

Yuri stepped in, carrying a plate and a bottle of something. He snapped on a light switch and the room came into full, overwhelmingly cluttered view. Tusker squinted up at him.

"I heard you wake up," Yuri said, matter-of-factly, as if nothing had happened. He set the plate down on top of a pile of old magazines on what Tusker assumed was a buried coffee table. It was a heap of steaming pirozhkis.

"Th-thanks," he said weakly, and reached for one.

"Careful, they're still hot," Yuri said, and walked over to a cupboard. He produced two small rocks glasses and set them down on the table. Both were filthy, with a rime of dust. Before Tusker could say anything, Yuri poured a healthy amount of the liquid into each.

"*Vashe zdorovye.*" He clinked his own glass against the

other, then drained it in one gulp. Tusker tentatively reached out and took the other glass, gave a sniff of its contents, then used the edge of his shirt to wipe the rim before taking a sip. It was ice cold and incredibly smooth, but very strong. He screwed up his face. Yuri exploded with laughter.

"You don't like my vodka?" he said, beaming and refilled his own glass.

"No, it's... it's actually very good," Tusker said and took another sip, this time draining his glass. "What kind is it? I'm not usually a vodka drinker, but this is amazing." Yuri reached over and topped off Tusker.

"I make it myself," he said, smiling proudly.

"You're serious?" Tusker said. He usually preferred his alcohol made from malted barley and aged in oak. Vodka all seemed to taste the same and never terribly interesting.

"I built a still many years ago, in the backyard here. Winters are long and it's a good way to pass the time." His face wrinkled up with a mischievous smile. "Plus, plenty of potatoes left over from the pirozhkis."

Tusker almost liked this guy, yet the way he'd shot Slider earlier removed any doubt that he was the trigger man who'd sent Overbrook's plane to the bottom of the lake.

"Earlier today," Tusker started to say, "the body..."

Yuri waved a big palm and shook his mane. "In the

freezer," he cut Tusker off. He dug in his pocket and pulled something out. It looked like a marble. He set it on the table and rolled it across to Tusker. It was Slider's prosthetic eye. Tusker recoiled in horror.

Yuri roared with laughter. "Proof of death!"

Tusker stared at it for a moment, then looked up at Yuri. "You put the body… in the freezer?"

"Yes, I have a freezer for my pirozhkis, but it's my off-season so not very full. It's about the size of a coffin. Very convenient."

"Wow," was all Tusker could say. Yuri gestured to the plate of pastries. Tusker looked at them differently now.

"Don't worry, those came out of the freezer before the body went in."

Tusker took one and had a bite. It was moist and chewy, with an earthy tang, and utterly delicious.

"Eat as many as you like," Yuri said, beckoningly. "They don't really keep well once they're baked."

Between mouthfuls, Tusker told Yuri everything that had happened up to that morning: his father's time in Vietnam, his dive on the Gulfstream, the meeting with Hockenheimer, Chester's clues. As he recounted it all, Yuri kept refilling their glasses. Tusker forgot about the pain in his ribs as he drank. By this time, it was 10:30 and his head was buzzing.

"So, this goon you killed was probably planning to finish you off, and me," he summarized.
"Until you shot her. How did you get to be such a good shot anyway?"

Yuri slammed back his glass again and loudly set it down on the table.

"I will tell you my story," Yuri said. "But first, we need another bottle."

When Yuri went to the other room to fetch more vodka, Tusker had an idea. He reached for his phone, quickly opened its voice recording app, pressed the big red "record" button, and set it discretely on the table behind a pile of old newspapers. Yuri returned with a fresh bottle of vodka and another plate of pirozhkis. He set them both down on the table, then settled into the tired old armchair opposite Tusker. He didn't seem drunk at all. His eyes were clear, and his tone became more serious as he began his side of the story.

"I was recruited as a boy by what was then the KGB. My father, I now realize, was working for them, extracting information from prisoners. He was not a nice man, though you asked how I became a good shot, and I guess I owe that to him." He shrugged and gave an ironic smile.

"I learned many skills. How to speak English, how to blend into American culture, how to handle weapons, how to make love for *kompromat*. Blackmail, you call it here." He spoke about all of this like someone reminiscing about college.

"Then they sent me to America. That was in 1970. My only orders were to 'blend in,' become a good American citizen, keep my head down, and wait until someone came for me. So I did. I missed Russia, but life in Michigan was good. It reminded me of my home on Lake Baikal." He paused and took a drink from his glass. Tusker couldn't believe what he was hearing.

"In early 1978… how do you say it? My number came up. I was living here, minding my business, thinking the KGB had forgotten about me. Then they came calling. This ex-Navy man, Hockenheimer, had been recruited by them." Yuri pronounced the senator's name slowly and deliberately. "They wanted to place him at the highest level of American government. But that senator…"

"Overbrook," Tusker filled in the name.

"Yes, that's him," Yuri said, then continued. "Overbrook was too powerful. They needed to eliminate him. So that summer, these men came over from Canada, KGB… They drove me across the border at Sault St. Marie, and we went many miles north, someplace no one would find us, and they trained me with this missile launcher—the Strela," he paused and smiled wistfully. "What a weapon. All you had to do was aim in the general direction of a target and it would do the rest. Just brilliant."

Tusker wasn't enjoying the story anymore. He was thinking of the plane at the bottom of the lake. Yuri continued.

"Then I was told to await word that the mission was to

proceed. They asked me to choose a code word, one they could use to alert me to proceed. I picked, 'sweetwater.' Did you know that in other languages, the opposite of saltwater is sweetwater? Damn English." He laughed.

Tusker chimed in. "So who gave this order? Was it Hockenheimer, or someone on his staff?"

"No no. That jackass is merely a... how do you say it? A puppet. Yes, this was planned in Moscow. Hockenheimer had nothing to do with the planning. But when he became senator, they made sure he knew who got him there."

It was all making sense now. Hockenheimer's leniency towards Russia. The proposed trade agreement. He'd been in their pocket all along. Tusker thought back to the *Navy Times* clipping of Lieutenant Hockenheimer shaking hands with a Russian attaché. And now he was poised to take the highest office in the land. There had been rumors of vote tampering, social media manipulation, and outright sabotage during the campaign, but shooting down a senator's airplane in the 1970s was irrefutable evidence. Or was it? A recording of an old Russian baker would be dismissed as fake news. Tusker needed something tangible.

"Would you be willing to speak publicly about this?" Tusker asked him, remembering his phone was recording the whole conversation.

Yuri bellowed. "Have you seen what Putin does to those who come out against him? I'll be drinking polonium tea before you know it."

Tusker was fuming. "You've enjoyed a good life here for decades. Where is your loyalty now? Still with the country that forced you to do terrible things? People need to know the truth!"

Yuri leaned forward in his chair and fixed Tusker with a glare. "I am loyal to one person—me!" He beat his own chest with his fist.

"You've got to give me something. If I hadn't come, you'd be dead already. You think that henchwoman yesterday was here to buy your pastries?"

"Well, that makes us even then," Yuri shot back. "You would be dead already if I hadn't shot her!"

They sat in silence for a long while. It was a stalemate. Yuri poured out more vodka. They'd been talking and drinking all night. The vodka had caught up with them both. Yuri was nodding off in his chair. Tusker was exhausted but he pressed on. He had one last idea.

"What did you do with the missile launcher?"

Yuri looked at him, then away towards the curtained window, as if seeing through it, out over the lake.

"It's out there." He pointed. Tusker half turned.

"Out where?"

"I threw it off the lighthouse."

"The Big Bay Lighthouse?"

"No," Yuri smiled. "Stannard Rock Lighthouse."

Tusker shuddered, thinking of that desolate place, wind whipped, waves crashing over it, out there in the dark. But he knew what he had to do.

"You don't happen to own a boat, do you?"

From Russia with Love

Lake Superior.
The next morning.

Three hours into the crossing, Tusker was convinced this was a bad idea. He almost told Yuri to turn back. In good weather, the boat, a 1968 Chris-Craft Commander, might have been up to the task. But the weather was not good. Neither was the boat.

It was clear to Tusker that Yuri had neglected the thirty-eight-foot cruiser. Its inside was even more cluttered than his apartment. There was visible evidence of rodent infestation, and what life jackets were on board were faded and torn. The engine took coaxing to start and sounded rough. A shame, thought Tusker, these boats were designed to handle rough water with deep-V hulls and spacious interiors. But it felt like a death trap on Superior in November.

Yuri kept the boat tied up to a rickety dock down a weed choked path behind his shop. There was a sheltered cove below the steep embankment, perfect for keeping a boat protected from weather. Tusker was surprised he'd never seen it from the water before, but the curve of the headland kept it hidden.

They left at first light. Tusker had slept only three fitful hours and woke up with a pounding head and his ribs aching. His mouth was dry, and he gulped down three quick cups of weak coffee in Yuri's kitchen. The two of them didn't talk much over a breakfast of leftover pirozhkis. It was hardly ample sustenance for what would likely be a very long and difficult day.

While Yuri went down to ready the boat, Tusker went out to the Scout to assess what dive gear he had in back. He was glad he'd tossed two steel air cylinders in to get refilled, but they were both only about half full after the Gulfstream dive. One of his backup regulators was jammed under the driver's seat. That was it. He hoped Yuri had some gear—a mask at least, maybe some fins. Everyone had those lurking in a garage, right?

Tusker shouldered one tank, hung the reg around his neck, and carried the other tank by its valve as he stumbled his way down the steep path to the dock. Every step caused stabbing pain in his chest and he arrived panting, his face bathed in sweat.

"Yuri, have you got any dive or snorkel gear of any kind?"

The big Russian stood on the transom, stroked his beard and frowned. Then he disappeared inside the boat again. Tusker could hear muttering and things being thrown around. A few minutes later, he emerged beaming, holding up a limp pile of ancient dive gear—a pair of baby blue Voit rubber fins, an oval mask, and a black and yellow rubber dive suit that looked like it would fit a gorilla. Tusker sighed. It would have to do.

Before they left the dock, Tusker took out his phone and sent an email to Leila, with the subject, "Sweetwater," and only one line: "See attached. Back tonight with more." Then he attached the audio file of his conversation with Yuri the night before and switched off his phone.

At 9:30 a.m., Tusker checked the GPS. They were just over halfway to Stannard Rock. The sky was a leaden gray, with low clouds that threatened rain, or snow. It sure felt cold enough for that. Yuri gripped the wheel and steered the old boat into successive swells. Tusker stood braced against the console, his feet wide apart, his eyes focused out the windscreen, where the wipers were no match for the constant spray. He almost couldn't believe he was out here again so soon, and he remembered the Gulfstream dive day just the week earlier, fighting down the sense of dread that was rising in him.

At one point, the engine seemed to falter, as if it had lost a cylinder or two. Yuri shouted for Tusker to take the wheel, then opened a hatch in the floor beneath the galley and disappeared below. The engine stopped. They were adrift, at the mercy of the building sea. Tusker did his best to keep the bow pointed into the waves, but it was no use without any power. Tusker glanced at the radio and hoped at least that worked in case they had to call for help. Then the engine fired again and the boat lurched forward. Yuri returned, wiping oily hands on the front of his pants.

"Clogged injector," he said calmly, and retook the wheel. He pulled a flask from his flannel shirt chest pocket and tipped it into his mouth.

"Is that really a good idea?" Tusker said, pointing to the flask.

Yuri smiled and held it out to Tusker, who shook his head. How could he drink at a time like this?

Just before noon, Yuri grunted and pointed at the horizon. Tusker squinted through the blurry windscreen. A flash of light. Stannard Rock loomed dead ahead. Tusker wasn't sure if he was happy or afraid to have arrived at the lonely light station. Having been empty since the sixties, it was no place for the living, especially on a stormy November day.

"You'll need to get on the bow and tie us up," Yuri said, gesturing out at the forward end of the Commander. Tusker pulled on his foul weather shell and a watch cap, then exited the relative comfort of the cabin to shimmy along the gunwales to reach the bow. Yuri throttled back the engine. The lighthouse loomed above them. Even the gulls were gone, Tusker noticed as he scanned the battered tower. The rock crib it stood on was coated in the white guano of the sea birds that made it their home all summer.

The boat slowly chugged up next to the crib. Tusker stood on the slippery bow, his feet wide, the bow line in his hands. As they neared the iron ladder that was bolted to the side, he reached across and grabbed it, pulling the Chris-Craft close, and looping the thick yellow nylon line around one of its sturdier-looking rungs. Yuri swung the boat so it was parallel to the wall and shouted something incomprehensible at Tusker through the windscreen.

Tusker knew what he was trying to do, and quickly moved aft along the side of the boat, pushing it away from the wall, and dropping a pair of lashed innertubes over the gunwale to protect the hull from the concrete. Then he continued aft and picked up a stern line. He searched the wall for anything to tie up to and spotted a rusty bollard. As Yuri continued to coax the boat, Tusker managed to loop the line around the bollard in a few figure-eights and tie it off.

"Secure!" he shouted. The engine went silent. They'd made it. Now it was time to dive.

Tusker jumped down onto the back deck of the boat and started to assess what he had to work with. The mask's rubber skirt was dried out and cracked and didn't fit Tusker's face very well. The fins were so old and loose they'd be difficult to swim in. Their blades were tiny compared to modern fins. Since Tusker didn't have neoprene dive booties, he'd wear his own woolen socks inside a pair of rubber fishing boots Yuri had on board, then jam his feet into the fins. The wetsuit was the biggest problem. It was at least three sizes too big for Tusker, and after zipping it up, it billowed like a limp garbage bag. He hoped it would provide enough buoyancy since he didn't have his harness and wing, but would be wearing his tank on his back rigged up with simple nylon webbing over his shoulders. This was a pitiful gear setup even in the best circumstances. But here in the bone chilling water of Lake Superior, looking for a four-decade-old object, it seemed ludicrous to even attempt it.

Yuri smoked a cigar as he watched him suit up, not

offering any help. Tusker struggled to find the right position for the tank with the webbing, and every time he shifted it, he felt his cracked ribs sting.

"So where do think you tossed the Strela?" Tusker asked him tersely. Yuri looked up at the lighthouse thoughtfully.

"Well, I remember I fired it from this side as the plane flew over to the south. Then I stepped over there," he pointed to the far side of the lighthouse crib. "No, wait a minute." He scratched his beard. "It was this side, yes, over here." He pointed to the exact opposite side now.

The lighthouse had been originally built to warn ships of Stannard Rock, a shallow shoal that rose up from the lake bottom. For about fifty feet surrounding the lighthouse crib, the water would be no deeper than twenty or thirty feet, sometimes as shallow as five or ten feet. Tusker was thankful for this. With half-empty air cylinders and no underwater torch, a shallow visual search was all he was equipped for, and even for that, not very well. But given Yuri's uncertainty, he might have to swim around the entire lighthouse looking for the damn thing. What were the chances it was still there? It could have been swept away into much deeper water during a storm. The lake drops off to over four hundred feet not far off the rock. Would it be covered in debris or algae?

Tusker closed his eyes and calmed himself. Then he puffed air from the mouthpiece, cinched the webbing as tightly as his ribs would bear, and pulled the mask straps as snugly as they would go, hoping it wouldn't leak too much. Then he nodded to Yuri, waddled awkwardly to the transom in the fishing boots and old blue fins, and stepped into the churning lake. At first, he sank like a rock before the buoyancy of the wetsuit pulled him back to the surface. Icy water immediately poured in through the neck seal and down into the boots. As Tusker turned one more time on the surface to orient himself to the lighthouse and the boat, he saw Yuri standing on the rear deck with an odd smile on his face. The last thing he saw as he descended was the name of the boat, painted in faded red across the stern: *From Russia with Love.*

The Strela

Stannard Rock Lighthouse.
The same day.

Despite the brooding, gray sky, underwater visibility was good. The shallow shelf of rock thirty feet below could even be seen from the choppy surface. The lake was simply too cold to support any organic matter other than a film of green algae that coated everything. The billowing wetsuit proved more buoyant than Tusker had anticipated, and it took a duck dive and several strong kicks with the old snorkeling fins for him to reach the bottom. Even then, he had to hold on to rocks and debris to keep from drifting up to the surface. The effort caused him to breathe hard, and with only the two half-empty tanks to work with, he didn't have a lot of time.

Yuri's ill-fitting, ancient mask leaked so much that it filled halfway with water by the time Tusker was able to clear it. *This will be a battle,* Tusker thought. He tried to develop a methodical rhythm: clear the mask, then pull himself along on the rocks one, two, three at a time. Scan for the missile launcher. Then start again — clear, pull, scan. He hoped Yuri had remembered correctly where he had discarded it. There was no way he could search around the entire lighthouse.

Tusker assumed there would be a fair number of artifacts here to sort through. Stannard had been a working, manned light station for close to a century. But he wasn't prepared for just how much junk had been discarded over the side. Coils of hose, crates, old tires, what looked like a generator, pipes, dozens of glass bottles, and fishing gear. Tusker had briefly researched what a Strela surface-to-air missile launcher looked like, but under the film of algae, any number of items looked like it. At one point, he pulled on a long cylindrical object he was convinced was the weapon, only to release a billow of silt and come away with a pneumatic speargun. Had the lighthouse keepers whiled away summer afternoons spearing burbots? He threw it away in frustration and cleared his mask again.

After forty-five minutes of this, Tusker was thoroughly chilled and had only covered about twenty square meters. He checked his pressure gauge, horrified to discover he had less than a hundred psi left in the first of his two tanks. At this depth, there was no decompression penalty, so it would be an easy swim to the surface, but he reminded himself to pay closer attention. He cleared the mask one more time, glanced around, and slowly ascended, breaking the surface just as he breathed the last cubic foot of air in the tank.

The boat was a fair swim away from where he surfaced, and Tusker struggled to swim to it. The waves cascaded off the lighthouse crib, and it caused a surge that pushed him away, so that for every two kicks with the pathetic fins, he was pushed back about three lengths. The rubber boots had filled up with water and he couldn't feel his toes anymore. He shouted for Yuri. There was no answer, and he wasn't at the stern of the boat anymore. Tusker cursed and swam harder, using his arms, which caused him to yelp with pain from his broken ribs.

With a final effort, his hand found the slippery hull of the boat. Since it wasn't set up to service divers, there was no ladder, so Tusker had to kick hard and pull himself awkwardly onto the transom. He lay there gasping and shivering for a long time, questioning why he was there in the first place. Then he thought of his father, how he'd nearly died not far from here, and how he kept two big secrets for the rest of his life.

"You OK?" It was Yuri's voice, shouting from above. Tusker opened his eyes and squinted up. The Russian was standing on the lighthouse crib, leaning over its rusted railing. The stub of the cigar was clenched in his teeth. With his wild beard, watch cap, and peacoat, he looked altogether like the portrait of a nineteenth century lighthouse keeper. Tusker raised a feeble hand.

"Just thought I'd climb up here for old time's sake," Yuri laughed.

Murderer, Tusker muttered to himself, and struggled to his knees, shedding the heavy steel cylinder, then the fins and mask, and throwing them onto the rear deck. His fingers were numb, his feet were numb, and he was shivering uncontrollably. He unzipped the wetsuit and pulled it off. He was wearing every layer of clothing he had underneath it, thankful he'd worn his pullover wool commando sweater, which retained a bit of warmth even while wet. He checked his watch: 2:30. Only about an hour and a half of daylight left. And maybe an hour's worth of air left in his remaining half tank. His prospects looked grim. Shivering, Tusker forced himself to swap his regulator over to the second tank, then wedged the empty one under some crates. He heard a thump on the bow and heavy footsteps. Yuri had climbed back down to the boat.

"No luck, eh?" He stated the obvious. Tusker just shook his head. He was huddled in a ball on one of the galley benches, a badly pilled acrylic blanket wrapped around him.

"I'll make some coffee," Yuri said. "But meanwhile, have some of this," he thrust out the flask of vodka. "Russian divers use it to keep warm," he smiled. Tusker didn't refuse this time, taking a long drink of the strong liquor. Yuri busied himself at the galley stove, heating water and scooping spoonfuls of instant coffee into a mug.

"Are you sure this was where you threw the missile launcher?" Tusker finally said.

"Well, when I was up there," Yuri gestured up to the lighthouse deck, "I remembered that I threw it off the side a little further that way." He pointed in the opposite direction from where Tusker had been diving.

"There's a lot of shit down there," Tusker said, annoyed. "If I had some proper diving gear, I might have a sporting chance of finding it."

"Hey, that was state of the art equipment when I got it," Yuri said defensively. "I cleaned the hull of the boat every summer with that outfit."

"Maybe in the 1980s," Tusker said. The kettle whistled and Yuri poured the water into the mug, then stirred it with a ballpoint pen. He handed the coffee to Tusker. It was weak and bitter, but it was hot, and he clutched the mug in both hands.

"Well, daylight's fading," Tusker said finally. "I'd better get on with it."

"You really think finding it will be enough to prove anything about Hockenheimer?" Yuri asked.

"It's one more piece of evidence," Tusker replied. "With the eyewitness testimony from seventy-eight, the underwater photos from my father's dive, and your story..."

"I'm not telling my story!" Yuri roared and slammed his empty mug down. "I take you to the Strela. That's all I can offer." He said this with finality.

Tusker paused. "It's too late, Yuri. I've already shared your story."

Yuri's face turned dark. "What do you mean, you 'shared' my story?"

"I recorded our conversation last night and sent it to a trusted friend. She can make sure the right people hear it.

You'll be safe, I promise."

"I can never be safe!" Yuri bellowed. "KGB never forgets. Putin never forgets." He paced the galley, banging his fist against the wood veneer cupboards. Tusker shifted uneasily. "You've just given me a death sentence!" He leaned over the galley table, spit flying as he spoke.

"Like you gave Overbrook and all the other passengers and crew on that plane!" Tusker shot back. "They didn't deserve to die. They were more innocent than you. And all the lies and coverups and false accusations all these years. Letting the truth out is at least a small measure of redemption."

Yuri went silent, turned and walked out of the galley, up into the wheelhouse. Tusker sat there in the fading light listening to the waves crash against the lighthouse and the boat. Perhaps he shouldn't have told Yuri, or at least waited until they were back on shore. It didn't matter. Now all that mattered was finding the missile launcher. He was filled with a sense of dread, thinking about climbing back into that cold, damp wetsuit and jumping into the lake again. But he did it anyway.

On the second dive, he swam around to the bow of the *From Russia with Love* to search the rocks on that side of the lighthouse. It was darker now and more difficult to differentiate objects below, especially through the constantly flooded mask. In order to combat his buoyancy, he'd tied a small folding anchor he'd found on Yuri's boat around his waist. It was awkward but added about eight pounds of ballast, and made staying close to the bottom easier—a small triumph.

Yuri had been no help before he got in the water. After their argument in the galley, he didn't emerge from the pilothouse, but sat in the dark, brooding. Now Tusker wondered if he could still trust the Russian. *No point dwelling on that now,* he thought, and cleared his mask once again.

His watch read 4:10 now, fifty minutes into the dive. It was almost fully dark. Without an underwater torch, he was reduced to searching almost by feel now. He didn't even want to think about the boat ride back. His pressure gauge read 100 psi. Maybe five minutes more air. As he crept forward, he felt a small tug at his waist. The grapnel anchor had somehow unfolded and snagged on something. Tusker reached back to release it but with his mask full, he couldn't find it.

The all too familiar sense of panic started to well up like a rising wave. *Calm down!* His numb fingers worked the rope around his waist, but it had become taut when the anchor got purchase. Fully blind now from the flooded mask, Tusker worked back down the rope, hand over hand to the anchor and found where it had fouled. He paused to clear his mask, which helped calm him, but it started to fill again immediately. He pulled at it. It budged slightly. He pulled again. A little more. But with the next inhalation, he sensed a difference. It was less satisfying and tasted vaguely metallic. He breathed again. Nothing. He was out of air.

Tusker pulled on the anchor with all the strength he

had left. He felt something stab in his chest as a broken rib pressed into his abdomen. The anchor came loose, sending Tusker tumbling. He scrabbled for something, anything to hold on to, and found something — a pipe — and clutched it. He had only a minute of consciousness left, maybe less. As he pulled himself back upright, it occurred to him that the tank and regulator were useless to him now. He wriggled out of them and dropped the cylinder on the rock. As he watched it fall away, he saw what he had grabbed. Could it be? His mask was nearly full of water now, but with the little oxygen in his bloodstream now, he managed to reach down and pick it up, then turn for the surface. As he did, he heard the rumble of an engine. It was unmistakable. He kicked hard for the surface, a mere ten feet above. He broke the surface with a gasp and threw off the mask just in time to see the *From Russia with Love* arc away from the lighthouse, churning south into the darkness.

The Loneliest Place on Earth, Revisited

In June of 1961, Stannard Rock Lighthouse caught on fire when gasoline in the storage shed exploded. The resulting inferno destroyed the shed and gutted the tower, even melting some of the limestone exterior. One man was killed, two others injured. The survivors were forced to wait on the exposed rock crib for three days, until a passing freighter saw their distress signal and radioed the Coast Guard for a rescue. The lighthouse was repaired but finally deemed too dangerous and remote and, in 1962, Stannard Rock Light was converted to an automated beacon. It has remained unmanned ever since.

Clutching the Strela in one frozen claw of a hand, Tusker climbed the slippery iron ladder to the lighthouse crib. It was dark now, and cold. Very cold. Tusker stumbled on the guano caked surface of the rock crib until he could find a bit of shelter from the wind behind the ruined shed next to the tower. He slumped to the ground in the wet diving suit and hugged his knees. He knew he had to get dry and warm soon, or he'd be fully hypothermic.

The longer I sit here, the sooner I'm going to die, he thought. *Then, none of this will matter. Yuri, the Strela, Hockenheimer.* He got to his feet and stripped off the wetsuit. The damp suit was only pulling heat away from his body now. He was wearing his woolen sweater on top, and only a pair of merino briefs, and he kept both on, along with his wool socks. The wind sliced through him. He had to get dry.

Tusker did a full two minutes of jumping jacks, gritting his teeth through the pain in his chest. Then he dropped down and pounded out thirty pushups. It might not be the best thing for cracked ribs, but he could feel warmth coming back into his body. His fingers started to burn as the blood flow returned. He decided to continue these exercises every ten minutes.

Staying warm was one thing, but finding some shelter was another. The obvious answer was right next to him: the lighthouse itself. While the concrete storage shed attached to the side of the tower provided some measure of cover from the wind, its windows and doors and much of its roof had been destroyed in the explosion of 1961 and never rebuilt. The tower would be better. A badly rusted staircase ascended from inside the shed to a doorway one level higher, on the side of the tower. Tusker cautiously started climbing it. A few of the steps were bent or missing entirely and he tested each one before committing his full weight.

At the top, the doorway to the tower's interior was sealed off with a piece of plywood. The Coast Guard maintained an automated beacon at the top of the tower, and though not many people came out this far in the lake, some attempt was made to keep out any curious fishermen who decided they might want a selfie atop "the loneliest place on Earth." Tusker leaned his shoulder against the plywood and gave a tentative push. It gave a little. He backed up as far as he could on the top step and took a short running start, ramming the wood panel. The impact jarred his ribs and he howled in pain, his scream carried away by the wind.

Reviewing his options, he decided it was the only way in. He gritted his teeth and, with a loud roar, thrust against the wood again. It splintered and gave way enough to get an arm inside. He reached in and pulled and pushed and tore at the plywood until he had enough of a gap to squeeze through. His wrist was bleeding and he'd gained a few splinters, but on the upside, he didn't feel cold anymore.

The inside of the tower was almost pitch black and smelled strongly of feces, or bird guano, or some sort of decay. The floor was covered in unseen debris. In only his socks, he stepped carefully, not wanting to stand on a nail. The dimmest of light emanated from a small window higher up, and Tusker moved towards it. A concrete staircase led up in a spiral around the perimeter of the tower and he climbed it, with one hand on the cold wall. He heard something scurry below. Were there rats way out here? Plenty of seabird eggs for them, Tusker reasoned, and continued climbing.

When he reached the window, the light showed what appeared to be a bathroom with two open toilet stalls. No point stopping here, Tusker thought, and kept climbing. He went up three more levels, past what seemed to be bunk rooms and another level of toilets, until he reached a more open space with some tables and a ruined chair. In the corner, on an outer wall, came a humming noise. A single red light glowed from an electrical box. This must be the power for the automated beacon atop the tower. Tusker slumped next to it, imagining that the batteries inside it were giving off a tiny bit of warmth. His ribs were a constant dull ache, his feet were raw and damp, and his hand was bleeding. Would anyone find him here? How often did the Coasties come to check on the tower? Yuri was long gone, Leila had no idea where he was. It was up to him to somehow signal for help. But how?

In 1961, the explosion and fire had knocked out the powerful light beacon. The survivors of the blast were forced to use their flashlights to signal for help, using the Fresnel lens atop the tower to amplify their light. It was another bit of Great Lakes lore familiar to so many in the region. Tusker thought about this, wondering if he could somehow do something similar. The Fresnel lens had long ago been removed and relocated to the maritime museum in Marquette. But there was still a beacon, a less powerful LED one. It might be enough to signal a passing freighter.

Tusker climbed the remaining spiral of stairs to the top of the lighthouse. Unlike the lighthouses of old, with their mechanical rotating lamps, the stack of eight sterile LEDs operated silently. It was eerie up there, 102 feet above the waves crashing at the rock crib below, darkness between the explosion of light every six seconds. The VLB-44 beacon system was rated for ten miles of visibility, hardly the equal of its incandescent predecessors. But then, modern commercial lake vessels didn't rely on Coast Guard aids for navigation anymore. Their pilothouses bristled with technology so that the massive ships locked onto GPS-guided courses and sailed virtually on autopilot.

Tusker knew all of this, but there would still be regular watches on board the freighters, and SOS signals were still well known to mariners. If only he could find a way to alter the six second flash of the beacon. Maybe the electrical box contained a clue. He descended the stairs and examined it. It was locked with a padlock and small hasp screwed into the access door. It wasn't anything particularly heavy duty, similar to the type used to lock shut a suitcase. He could probably smash the lock, or pry the hasp. Looking around for any obvious tools at hand, he picked up a broken chair in the room and managed to break off one of its spindle legs. Using it like a hammer, he swung again and again at the lock. It didn't give, and the dried-out wood of the chair leg splintered and disintegrated in his hand.

Then, an idea crossed his mind: his watch. The Seiko, with its heavy steel case, could be used as a hammer to break the lock, or at least bend the hasp enough to pull it loose. He slid the bracelet off his wrist and over his hand. He closed his eyes, remembering how Samanthi had given it to him the last time he saw her. He pictured it on her wrist when they dove together in Sri Lanka, how she never took it off, even when they made love. Then he smiled. She would probably laugh at the thought of him being in yet another impossible predicament, and likely approve of him using her old watch as a tool.

He held the watch by its bracelet and threaded it through his knuckles so that the case hung slightly away. Then he took aim and swung the watch down at the lock, softly at first to practice, then again, harder and harder. A few times he caught his knuckle on the lock and cried out. But he kept hammering. The timing ring of the watch flew off, pinging somewhere in the darkness onto the floor. He swung again, then paused to examine its effect on the padlock. The lock itself didn't show any sign of giving, but the steel loop of the hasp had started to bend and pull free. Progress. He aimed and swung the watch again. This time, the glass crystal flew off. The Seiko was utterly destroyed, but the lock was almost loose. One more good hit. The latch popped open, and the padlock hit the floor with a thud. He was in.

Tusker squatted down and squinted into the box. There was a row of small rechargeable batteries lined up, with cables connecting them together, then two stouter cables that passed through a rubber grommet on top of the box. Tusker traced them. One likely brought power from the solar panels outside the lighthouse and the other sent power to the beacon above. He couldn't see a way to alter the beacon's flash sequence, likely programmed remotely for simple six-second intervals.

"Damn it!" Tusker cursed out loud. It was like modern cars. *No way to work on them yourself anymore,* he thought, remembering the night with Carl getting the Scout running. It seemed so long ago now. He wished Carl was with him now. He'd surely know what to do.

With his watch destroyed, Tusker had no way of knowing what time it was, but he guessed it was close to 10 p.m. He was getting cold again, and he stood up to do more jumping jacks, but only managed a few before he got tired. When was the last time he'd eaten anything, or had any water? What he'd give for even a small campfire.

That was it — fire! It was a risk, sure, but would certainly get attention if he could build one big enough. Down on the crib would be too hidden from view. But up high, even atop the tower itself, would almost surely be seen by passing vessels, or even aircraft descending into Marquette.

With a plan in mind, Tusker felt a surge of energy and made the most of it. First, he'd need plenty of dry fuel. Remembering the plywood of the boarded-up door, he scrambled down the flights of spiral stairs, all the way to the bottom, taking less care than before. He found the plywood he'd broken and tore off as many more pieces as he could, then snapped them into smaller pieces he could carry. He made a pile at the foot of the stairs, and when he was done, started carrying armfuls up in multiple climbs to the tower. The effort made him sweat, and he was panting from the exertion. His ribs ached, his mouth was dry, and his feet were blistered and raw, worn right through his wool socks. He cursed his recent cigarettes and the vodka, vowing to get back in shape when — if — he made it out of this alive.

In the top of the tower, in the eerie flash of the beacon, Tusker built a lattice of wood, with smaller pieces in the bottom for kindling. From a rat-chewed mattress he found in one of the sleeping quarters two levels below, he tore some foam to use for tinder and stuffed it beneath his makeshift wood pile. He hoped once the fire got big enough, it might catch the window frames and then the wood flooring, creating an inferno, fed like a chimney by air coming up the drafty tower. Now all he needed was a way to ignite it. For that, he already had an idea.

Tusker examined the LED beacon. The power cable plugged into the base of the stack. He pulled on it and after some resistance, it popped free. The flashing stopped and he briefly wondered if the Coast Guard had some way of monitoring it, and would get an alert if it stopped. He doubted it and anyway couldn't take the risk of waiting. He stripped back the insulation on the cable with his raw fingers, exposing the wires inside. One was power, one was ground. In the dark, he had no way of telling them apart. But all he needed to do now was connect them with a piece of metal and it would create a spark to ignite some tinder. He gathered a tuft of the foam from the mattress and flattened it on the edge of the beacon platform, then laid his ruined watch on top of it. He touched the two exposed ends of the power cable to the steel bracelet of the watch. There was a brief spark, then an acrid smell. Tusker bent and blew on the foam. A flame licked up and quickly began to consume the foam. He picked it up and it burned his fingers, but he ignored the pain and was able to drop it in the bottom of his wood pile. Then he gently blew into it until a steady flame rose and ignited the wood.

Within a few minutes, the fire had consumed most of the plywood, which was damp and billowing white smoke. The warmth felt good, and the orange light lent some comfort, but without more wood, he had nothing else to burn. After all, the point wasn't comfort, but visibility. He needed a big fire. Tusker extracted a burning board and held it up against the top of a window frame. It caught, and flames began to lick higher. Soon a roof timber started to hiss and pop. Then, suddenly, the entire roof of the lighthouse was on fire. Time to go.

Tusker took one last look around before racing down the stairs, slipping and nearly falling head first, until he reached the kitchen and the door to the ruined storage shed. It seemed counterintuitive to leave the relative warmth and shelter of the tower, but if the fire grew, it would quickly consume the entire structure.

Tusker took shelter in the far corner of the ruined shed. He looked up at the burning tower above him. It was a surreal sight, like a huge medieval torch burning in the night sky. Ash and burning embers rained down on him and he smelled smoke on the swirling wind. He had no strength left and began to drift in and out of consciousness, trying to fight the urge to sleep. But in the end, it was a losing battle. Finally, with the entire lighthouse glowing in flames, he cradled the damp wetsuit and the Strela against his chest and closed his eyes.

The Gales of November

Peninsula Medical Center, Marquette, Michigan.
Two days later.

When he was told about it later, Tusker thought it fitting that it was the pilot of an airplane who spotted the fire on Stannard Rock. It was a small commuter flight from Houghton descending into Marquette. The pilot called it in to the control tower. The Coast Guard was alerted and sent a helicopter and the buoy tender *Spar* to the scene.

Tusker didn't remember the Sikorsky MH-60 Jayhawk helicopter hovering over the burning lighthouse crib, or the rescue swimmer descending on a cable to haul him up, but he was later told that he refused to let go of the oddly shaped algae-covered cylinder he was clutching when he was winched from the flaming lighthouse to the chopper, before being flown to Peninsula Medical Center.

The fire burned for two days and the Coast Guard didn't even attempt to extinguish it. The expense and hazard of fighting the flames was not justified, and ultimately a new beacon on a simple steel platform could replace it. Besides, the weather had deteriorated overnight into a Force 10 storm, kicking up twenty-foot seas and snow squalls.

The first thing Tusker heard as he regained consciousness was Leila's voice. He smiled and opened his eyes, but there, hovering over him, wasn't Leila. It was Carl.

"Well, damn. And here I thought I was gonna inherit your Scout."

"Nice to see you too, pal," Tusker said weakly. He tried to sit up but fell back against the hospital bed.

"Easy now, tiger." It was Leila, who approached from behind Carl. Her tough demeanor was softened, and her eyes showed concern. She bent to kiss him softly on the lips.

"I'd tell you to get a room but... well, we're already in one," Carl quipped.

"What... what happened? The election, Yuri... Did you publish your story?" Tusker's words flowed out in a hurried jumble. He'd been in and out of consciousness for two days after being rescued. Leila put her finger to his lips.

"All in good time," she said. "You need rest right now. Rest assured, things are in motion."

"At least tell me they found Yuri."

"They found his boat," she said, looking at the floor. "It was washed up on the shore east of Pictured Rocks. No one aboard. The Coast Guard presume he fell overboard."

Tusker looked up at Leila. "He's alive, you know. They'll never find him. He's long gone, I know it."

"Well, the important thing is, we got his story, and apparently his apartment has been a treasure trove of evidence."

Tusker thought of Slider's body in the freezer and shuddered.

"What happened to the Strela?"

"The what?"

"The missile launcher! It made it back, didn't it?"

"Oh, yes, it did. I handed it over to the FBI, but don't worry, I took a lot of photos of it before I did."

Tusker smiled. The TV was on in the room, its volume muted. He could see the smiling face of Ted Hockenheimer with a caption underneath: "President-elect faces questions." Tusker's eyes grew wide and he tried to sit up, but fell back with a shout of pain.

"Wait, he... he won?" He pointed at the TV.

"A country gets the leaders it deserves," Carl said slyly. "No thanks to your vote, you indifferent slacker."

"At least I had a good excuse," Tusker said weakly. "But what's the latest? I thought for sure..."

Leila sat gently on the edge of the bed and laid a hand on Tusker's leg, as if to comfort him.

"It was closer than anyone expected," she said. "A few states are holding recounts. But there's already talk of an inquiry and Congressional hearings into the '78 plane crash."

"They're calling it, 'Hocken-gate.'" Carl chimed in, smiling. He was picking at the plate of food a nurse had left for Tusker.

"More like 'Sweetwatergate'," Tusker quipped, pleased with his own joke. "Is there any way he can survive this? The guy is like a cockroach."

"I don't think so," Leila replied. "My story broke the morning of the election, so a little too late to affect things. Of course, Hockenheimer's already calling it 'fake news,' and saying that Yuri was a figment of the opposition's imagination, but once the missile evidence is made public…"

"Saving the best part for last," Tusker said, smiling up at her.

"More like I wanted to make sure all the Ts were crossed," she replied. "Yuri's story was a bombshell, but I didn't want to blow my wad, so to speak, with the missile until there was more firm evidence. The FBI is promising to analyze your father's photos, the Strela you found, and maybe even re-examine the wreck."

"I wish them luck," Carl chimed in. "You won't get me out there diving that plane again. Last time..." He cut himself off, casting a sheepish glance at Tusker.

"Don't worry, pal, once was enough for me too," Tusker said gently. "Anyway, I need some warm water diving for a change." He looked at Leila. "Want to come to Mexico with me? I've got a project coming up in the Yucatán."

"I'd love to," she said softly, and kissed him on the mouth.

The Road Home

Marquette, Michigan.
Late November.

From his supine position on the leather sofa, Tusker could see the top of a maple tree out the window. It was swaying back and forth silently, most of its leaves stripped by the late November wind.

"You seem different this week," Dr. Fuchs said. "More… content, perhaps?" They'd been talking for twenty minutes and Tusker had filled her in on some, but not all, of what happened since they'd last met.

"Don't read too much into things, Doctor Freud," Tusker said, sitting up on one elbow. "I'm only lying down because of my damn broken ribs." He'd chosen to lie on the leather sofa in the therapist's office this week. Dr. Cassandra Fuchs laughed out loud. It brightened her face, Tusker thought, softened the edges of her clinical demeanor. She was again wearing a fitted turtleneck—black today—and he wondered if she owned any other type of clothing.

"You don't lead a terribly quiet life, do you? It seems you inherited your father's thirst for adventure, at the very least."

Tusker chuckled. “You could say that, although I’m ready for some quiet time, I think.”

“So, what did you learn about your father since we last met?” She switched back to her serious tone. “I’d asked you to revisit some of his things, explore his past a little.”

“He was a more complicated person than I guess I ever knew,” Tusker replied, smiling. He laid back on the sofa, wincing as he did.

“Most of us are,” she replied without looking up from the notepad on which she was scribbling. Then she paused and made eye contact. “Does this realization open the door to… forgiveness?”

“It’s too late for that, isn’t it?” Tusker said. “Anyway, it’s not really from me that he needed forgiveness.” He didn’t go into more detail. The doctor let the remark pass.

“Do you see any similarities between you and him?”

“Perhaps,” Tusker swiveled his legs around and sat up with a grimace. “We both experienced some traumatic episodes and moral gray areas. I just wish I didn’t have to find out about his by going through my own.”

“Sadly, that’s often the case,” Dr. Fuchs said, reaching for a steaming mug of herbal tea on the table next to her. “The important thing is that you learn from it.”

“I think I’ve done enough learning for a while.”

"And this woman you've met. How is that going? Are you able to open up to her about some of your feelings?"

Tusker thought of Leila. She was going to meet him at the cabin that evening after one last run on her motorcycle. Tusker had offered to let her park it in the shed for the winter. It had been almost a week, and he was surprised at how much he missed her smile, her hands, her lithe body.

"Julian?" Dr. Fuchs interrupted his thoughts.

"Sorry," Tusker blushed, then looked across at her.

"I'm glad it's going so well." She smiled and winked, then glanced at her watch. "That about does it for this session. Do you want to keep next week's time?"

"You know, doc, I think I'm good."

She nodded. "I think you are too. But I'm here if you ever want to resume our chats." She said it almost wistfully, as if she would miss him.

"Thanks." Tusker smiled, stood up slowly, shook the doctor's hand, and left the office.

Any hope of late season warmth was long gone now. Late November in the U.P. was as good as winter, and the first snow was in the forecast for the weekend. It was arriving late this year. As Tusker climbed into the Scout, he made a mental note to source some winter tires. Carl would know where to get some.

The engine fired on the first turn of the key and Tusker waited a minute while it warmed up, then closed the choke halfway before pulling away from the curb. The old truck was running well now. It made him think of his father, and how pleased he'd be to see the old Scout back on the road. He smiled and rubbed the dashboard affectionately. It was faded and cracked from summers of hot sun. The passenger seat vinyl was cracked, its stuffing showing through. The corner of the windscreen sported a Michigan State Parks permit sticker from 1976, and he imagined his parents driving downstate, a canoe strapped to the roof, for some camping on the beach.

On the outskirts of Marquette, he remembered he was supposed to pick up a bottle of wine to share with Leila and he pulled into a small liquor store. Wine wasn't really his thing, but Leila was on her motorcycle, so he had offered to stop and find something.

"No promises," he'd told her on the phone.

"No expectations," she'd replied. "Just find something that'll get us drunk."

He came out with a twelve dollar bottle of merlot that the person at the shop said was good, and slid into the Scout, stuffing the bottle in his bag. It was only three-thirty but it was already getting dark. As he waited to turn onto the highway, a state trooper raced past, its lights flashing, followed by an ambulance. That can't be good, he thought, and pulled out to follow, heading west.

The old radio in the Scout only received AM stations. As

he drove, Tusker fiddled with the dial to find something — country music, sports talk show, oldies. He settled on the news that, these days, was still all about the election and the president-elect's questionable past.

"Sore loser," a Hockenheimer spokesperson was calling the defeated incumbent. "It's time for this country to move beyond petty finger pointing, 'gotcha' journalism, and fake news. President-elect Hockenheimer has a country to rebuild, and that doesn't start with dragging up past rumors."

Tusker switched it off. Up ahead in the twilight, he saw a line of brake lights and the red and blue flicker of emergency vehicles. Deer strike? Drunk driver? He downshifted the Scout and coasted to a crawl behind a minivan. He checked his watch. His Seiko was somewhere out on Stannard Rock now, shattered and probably melted into the rock from the fire. He'd taken to wearing Chester Basch's old Tudor. Now it read close to four thirty. The traffic crept forward, getting closer to the scene. Drivers were slowing to catch a glimpse of someone else's bad day.

A trooper in a fur collared jacket and stocking cap was directing traffic around some road flares. The minivan pulled away and the trooper waved for Tusker to pull through. In the beam of his headlamps and the glow of the flares, he made out the ugly smear of rubber on the pavement and some sort of liquid. Motor oil? Fuel? Then, he saw it. There, on the shoulder, where the gravel disappeared into tall grass, with the dark woods beyond, the unmistakable shape of a motorcycle lying on its side.

It had a red gas tank, and its handlebars were twisted up at an odd angle.

"No!" Tusker shouted out loud. He felt his skin go cold. He pulled the Scout off the road, despite the shouts from the trooper, who told him to keep driving. Tusker left the engine running and jumped out, now sprinting over to the upturned bike. As he approached it, he could make out the Royal Enfield logo. There, next to it, was a canvas dispatch bag and a familiar full-face helmet. Tusker felt his legs go weak, and he fell to his knees, feeling the urge to vomit.

"You need to get back in your vehicle and move along, sir." The trooper was standing over him. Tusker just stared at the wreckage. "Now!"

He looked up at the trooper. "I… I know this person. Is she OK?"

The cop gave him an odd look, then glanced up and across the road. Tusker's eyes followed, and he saw the ambulance. The back doors were open, and in the harsh white light cast from inside, he could see a stretcher being loaded. On it was what looked like a large black duffel bag. Someone was zipping it shut.

"I'm sorry, sir," the trooper finally said. Tusker searched his face. "Looks like a hit and run, judging by the debris and…"

Tusker wasn't listening anymore. He got to his feet in a daze and slowly walked back to the Scout. Its rich smelling exhaust was swirling in the red glow of its tail lamps. He climbed in behind the steering wheel and stared ahead, into the late autumn darkness. There was the faintest red in the sky, the last light of the day. A deer was looking back at him, its eyes catching a reflection of the Scout's headlamps. Then it disappeared into the forest. Tusker closed his eyes and wept.

Epilogue

Theodore Hockenheimer was sworn in as President of the United States on an unusually warm January morning in Washington. In his first speech after taking office, he vowed to restore trust to the highest office in the land and regain America's position as a world leader. He made no mention of Michigan, the state he represented in the Senate since 1978. Instead, he told an anecdote about being a "kid born in New Jersey."

A week after the inauguration, the FBI opened an investigation into the circumstances surrounding the crash of Senator Clay Overbrook's plane in Lake Superior. In addition to interviews with witnesses and photographic analysis, the bureau, in cooperation with the U.S. Navy, attempted to salvage the crashed Gulfstream. But the weather and sea conditions were deemed too dangerous in December for diving, and the operation was postponed indefinitely.

The Strela missile launcher discovered at Stannard Rock Lighthouse was lost in transit to an FBI laboratory.

Yuri Sokolov was never found, dead or alive. The Coast Guard officially declared him 'lost at sea, presumed dead.' His former pirozhki shop in Big Bay, Michigan was bulldozed, and today an RV campground stands on its former location. It is called Sweetwater Campground.

Leila Mansour won a posthumous Pulitzer for investigative journalism. Her parents accepted the award on her behalf. Her father died of a broken heart two months later. The *Detroit Free Press* announced a scholarship for aspiring women journalists in Leila's name. Her follow up story about the Strela was never published.

Six months after the election, President Hockenheimer signed an historic trade agreement with Russia. The first tanker of Russian crude oil arrived in the Gulf of St. Lawrence two weeks later. Its final destination: the Great Lakes Refinery, north of Detroit.

Stannard Rock Lighthouse was rebuilt by a nonprofit preservation society, thanks to an anonymous donation of one million dollars. It remains the loneliest place on Earth.

Acknowledgements

Sweetwater came together a lot faster than my first novel did. I owe some of that to my own knowledge and discipline, picked up from writing *Depth Charge*. But also, I had a lot of help with this one.

Ladric Grant provided valuable plot ideas and poked holes in others during the summer when the story took shape, and our conversations in the garden over curry dinners were invaluable.

Suresh Hettiarachchi went above and beyond, with his in-depth knowledge of aviation and flight paths, contributing to the all-important prologue.

Brian Palmer, US Coast Guard Chief Aid to Navigation (ATON) Officer at Sault St. Marie, was kind enough to provide details about the light station at Stannard Rock.

Tadzio Bervoets lent valuable feedback about Tusker's sojourn in Jamaica, from fishing techniques to wildlife to traditional breakfasts.

Doug Swanson not only provided valuable information about International Harvester Scouts, but even allowed me to see his vintage truck and took me for a spin on a lovely Minnesota summer evening.

Pascal Balesi, United States Navy Master Chief (retired), lent his expertise to the Navy diving chapters, giving some authenticity to an area of which I had little knowledge.

My good friend, the Great Lakes maritime historian Chris Winters, reviewed the manuscript for accuracy as it pertained to all things shipwrecks and Lake Superior.

Benjamin Lowry, former commercial diver and Coastie, weighed in on the salvage attempts on the Gulfstream. His feedback made the chapter, "Red Diver, Blue Diver" much stronger.

My friend and colleague James Stacey deserves thanks for his years of support in my efforts, not only with this book but also with *Depth Charge*.

Tom Bushey is a longtime Michigander, who's not only lived on Lac La Belle but also went to Michigan Tech, where Tusker teaches. His input on everything from geography to flight paths to suggesting the Seney Stretch for the "Night Driving" chapter made the story so much richer.

When I first announced *Sweetwater*, an author and book reviewer, Michael O'Donnell, reached out with some good advice about publishing and encouraged me to pursue traditional publishing for this book. He even introduced me to his literary agent, a shortcut many authors would love to have. I appreciate all his advice and feedback and the time he took to talk to me about the frustrations and hopes of being a fiction author.

And that agent he introduced me to? Paul Feldstein in

Belfast, who worked with me to edit the manuscript for what turned into the book you're reading. Paul was kind and professional and worked to pitch my manuscript to dozens of publishers before I pulled the plug and decided to once again self-publish. It was a learning experience and I greatly appreciate the time and effort Paul put into my work. I hope I can work with him again, if he'll have me.

Paul Andrews once again lent his talent to the cover design and typesetting of *Sweetwater*. It's been one of the joys of writing and publishing this book, and *Depth Charge,* to work with Paul, who so perfectly captured the tone of the stories in his designs.

Chris Sohl was the right person to proofread *Sweetwater*. His attention to detail and knowledge of diving and history were invaluable, but more importantly, he's become a trusted friend and confidant. His work on the book improved it considerably.

Finally, to my family, I am eternally grateful—my parents, who have always been behind my work, however whimsical and questionable, are a lifelong source of encouragement and support, in every way possible.

And to Gishani, who might as well be listed as a co-author for all the hours she put into hashing out plotlines, reviewing chapters, and being a steadfast rock of support, through what is, admittedly, a dalliance. I love you and owe you all my success.

About the Author

Jason Heaton has over a decade-long history of adventure, travel, wristwatch, and gear writing. His work has appeared in *Outside* magazine, *Gear Patrol, Men's Journal, The Telegraph, Wired, Australian Geographic,* and *Hodinkee,* among others. In 2017, *The New York Times* called him "a test pilot for the world's most illustrious undersea timepieces." He is the co-host of the popular podcast, *The Grey NATO,* and creator of the blog, *Swimpruf.* In 2021, he published his first novel, *Depth Charge.*

A certified technical diver, Heaton has been underwater all over the world, from the Galapagos to New Zealand to the Caribbean and, since 2015, he has been a member of the prestigious Explorers Club. He lives with his wife, Gishani, in Minneapolis.

Made in the USA
Las Vegas, NV
06 November 2023